ACROSS THE PLANE

Tom Carpenter's Journey

By

JAKE PIXLEY

ACROSS THE PLANE

ISBN: 978-1544837062

CHAPTER 1

For most people in the small town of Beachwood, on those midsummer days of 1999; life just moved along like any other day. For most people life moved on, but not all. On Dogwood street, house number four one five; life for one man seemed to have come to a halt. From the street it appears much like any other house. It was a basic three bedroom two bath, single story house with white vinyl siding and black trim. The yard was well trimmed with a small waterfall and goldfish pond with the sidewalk wrapping around it. A hedge grew on each side separating this house from the next one down the street. What made this place so different from all the rest in the neighborhood was who and what was inside of it.

The things inside were grief, sorrow and the pain memories often bring with them. Inside the house, the television was on in the living area with a local weatherman giving his report. Just passed the living area to the right; a double door opening led into the kitchen area, where the who of this story, Tom Carpenter was sitting at the dining table. Tom was a man in his forties, medium build, clean shaven and coal black hair. He was a good looking man and carried himself as a self-made and self-respecting man.

On this particular morning, Tom was dressed as if he were fixing to go into work. He had on his work boots, blue jeans and a grey denim long sleeve shirt that had his name on the right front above the pocket and the title of superintendent on the other. Tom was dressed for work due to habit, but he had no intentions of going, and somewhere deep inside he knew it. He knew it, because this day was no different than any other.

Tom sat at the first chair down from the end of a long western design kitchen table with six chairs eating the breakfast made of eggs, bacon, a biscuit and some gravy he had cooked. Although he sat alone, his plate wasn't the only one on the table. He had prepared another plate and sat it on the other side of the table directly across from him. Beside the other plate was a picture of a woman with sandy blonde hair, green eyes and a beautiful smile. It was clearly a studio photo with the dark blue background, but it was also one of Tom's favorites of the woman he once knew as his wife.

At one point during his breakfast, Tom stopped eating and looked at the photo of his wife with a saddened look on his face as he said. "I still can't get use to cooking for myself. I always cook too much. Wherever you are sweetie, my Kristi, whenever you get home, I'll be here waiting for you."

After breakfast Tom cleaned the dishes and wiped down the table, just as he had been doing for several weeks as he waited for the return of his wife. When everything was clean he took the photo back to his bedroom and placed it on the nightstand beside his bed. Just like every other morning, day and evening; Tom sat in his leather recliner with his feet up watching TV. No matter how long he sat there, he never changed the channel and no remote appeared to be anywhere in sight.

Every once in a while, Tom would look away from the TV as if he were seeing or remembering someone on the leather couch now covered with a sheet. Tom would get a slight smile on his face but it didn't last. Each time after those brief moments his face would sadden and he would return to watching TV.

Every evening just like every other evening just as it began to get dark outside; Tom would get up and go take a shower in the master bathroom connected to his bedroom. Afterwards while in his plane cotton pajamas and bathrobe, Tom would make his way to different bedroom of the house.

This room was just passed the living area and front door of the house, and first door on the left of the hallway which led to a guest bedroom and bathroom. Upon entry of the first door on the left it was clear it was a girl's room. The room walls were painted a dark almost red colored pink and many posters of boy bands and other music stars were pinned up. Next to the walk in closet was a desk covered with multiple types of makeup and a couple brushes along with a large mirror with a few photos of people.

Tom walked over to the mirror and rubbed his thumb across the face of a teenage brunette girl in a photo that looked like it was taken for a year book as it had the year 1992 on the bottom of it. As Tom rubbed the photo he said out loud in the room. "I love and miss you, my sweet girl." Afterwards Tom walked over and kneeled by the bed covered in what most would consider too many pillows, and topped with a light green comforter. Just sticking out in view from the comforter was the head of a white teddy bear.

Just like every other night, Tom pulled the teddy bear out from the cover and held it close. It was an odd looking teddy bear because it wasn't round and plump like most. It was very skinny except for the head. It was a valiant effort by Tom to try and make a teddy bear, but it turned out looking like a sock monkey with a teddy bear head. Either way, it was his daughter's favorite toy since she was a baby, and it was her who named it Skinny.

While holding the teddy bear, Tom said. "I miss you Amy... My beautiful baby girl." After a moment of kneeling silently, Tom put the skinny teddy bear back under the cover with its head sticking out, and he left the room. Tom made his way back to the kitchen to fill his mug stamped #1 Dad with water from the sink and then he went to his bedroom. Tom sat the mug on his night stand while he got a woman's shirt out of the hamper in the closet. He held the shirt to his nose, took a deep breath and walked back over to his bed and began putting his pillow inside the body of the shirt. Tom was the kind of man that would never want anyone to see him do that, and he surely wouldn't ever tell. To Tom, putting the worn shirt of his wife which carried her scent around his pillow made him feel closer to her.

Tom got into bed and laid down with the right side of his face on the shirt covered pillow, he looked to an enlarged photo on the wall of him with his wife and daughter by a lake. In the photo they were all smiling and obviously happy. Though Tom liked seeing and remembering them with smiles on their faces; it also saddened him that he could no longer be next to them. The closest he could seem to get was with old clothes carrying their scent which he refused to wash, and a teddy bear that looked like a sock monkey. With his left eye barely open and somewhat teary, Tom whispered while looking at the photo and falling asleep. "I can't make it without you two."

Soon after his whispering words of sorrow Tom fell asleep. For Tom, that night was just like all the other nights of the last several weeks. Tom rolled all over the bed as dreams of painful times passed began gripping him. In his dreams the scene of the police standing at his front door telling him and his wife their daughter died in a car accident played over and over. In other scenes of his dreams, Tom would see the smile on his daughter's face when she first got her driver's license. Then the dream would go back to the police, and family saying how sad it was for a girl to die just two weeks after getting a license. Other dreams were about the time right after the wreck when Tom contemplated killing the other driver who was drunk that night and hit his daughter head on. Deep down, Tom regretted not doing it, but had to be there and be strong for his wife Kristi.

Other dreams were at the funeral after all others had left the cemetery, except Tom and Kristi who stood watching as the casket was lowered in the ground. Each night, like every other night as Tom had these dreams; he saw brief flashes of bright light and sometimes the inside of a hospital room. He could only imagine it was from his stay at the hospital after his wreck just a little while back.

The dreams and flashes of light often woke Tom with the wonder of why his wife had died when he was the only one in the car when he wrecked. He couldn't figure out how she was gone when he knew she was home. Tom couldn't remember how he got home from the hospital either. The last he remembered was the light over his head in the hospital room and he fell asleep to later wake up in his own bed with no one else there. Most of the situation with Kristi was a mystery to Tom. And it was a mystery he was afraid to find the answer to. To him, it was better to believe she would return, than to confirm she never would.

Tom's love for his wife and daughter put things in motion that he would have little control over. The truth will always refuse to stay hidden for too long. Tom Carpenter went to sleep believing with all his heart, he must stay in that house on Dogwood Street until his wife come back home. To him, it was where he belonged. However; someone else had different plans. Someone else was on the way down the street to change Tom Carpenter and his life forever.

CHAPTER 2

Come daylight the next morning, Tom got out of bed and continued with same routine he had been doing. He got dressed for work and went in the living area carrying his #1 Dad mug with him to turn on the TV to make a racket while he cooked breakfast. Once the TV was on, Tom went into the kitchen and got the coffee started while he began cracking eggs in a bowl.

During the mixing of the eggs, milk

and seasoning; Tom said to himself. "God I wish they were here." Unlike most people, it never got easier for Tom. His sadness and longing for his wife and daughter never eased. Looking at the photos of him with his family and the appearance he had at this time the difference in his face was staggering. He looked so tired, hurt and almost as if he could fall over dead at any time.

With the eggs, bacon and biscuits done and the gravy on the final stir, Tom turned off the stove and got two plates out of the cabinets to set the table. Tom didn't set at the head of the table, but rather one seat down on the right and he set the other plate directly across from him on the left. Both were set with matching cloth napkins, a cup of coffee, fork and knife. Tom knew it wasn't normal behavior to set a plate for someone who was gone, but he couldn't give up. He had to believe at some point, his wife Kristi would come through the door.

Tom sat down and bowed his head for a silent prayer for just a moment. When he was done with his prayer, he took a sip of coffee, picked up his fork and began to cut into the gravy covered biscuits when there was a knock at the front door. Tom's heart began to race; the sudden noise and surprise of something different spooked him a little. Deep inside he was hoping it was his wife, but truthfully he had no idea who would be knocking when no one had since he come home from the hospital.

Tom gazed at the door in almost disbelief of what he heard and unsure it actually happened, when again there was a knock at the door. Tom got up slowly with a look of suspicion on his face and he eased over to the door. His heart was pounding as he couldn't imagine if he could handle it if it were his wife standing on the other side; but he had to take the chance. Tom opened the door and who he saw certainly was not his wife. It was a woman, but it was an old woman known in the town as the crazy old psychic woman.

She lived on the outer edge of town in the middle of a brushy field in an old run down house. The kids in the area called the place haunted and declared her a witch as kids are known to do. Her name was Evelyn Murray. She appeared to be in her late sixties or early seventies with long dark grey hair that hanged down on the sides of her face, and didn't appear to have any teeth, or false teeth from the look of her jaws clenched together. She had a medium size frame, deep eye sockets and wore a dark grey poncho over her very faded red and white striped muumuu. Her facial features give her the appearance of a woman who had great knowledge, life experience or great insanity.

Tom asked the woman. "How can I help you?" The old woman smiled at Tom and said with her slow raspy voice. "No you cannot. I am here to help you Tom Carpenter." Tom looked around outside for a moment and then replied. "Well I don't need any help, but if you like, I can take you back home so you don't have to walk." The old woman asked Tom. "Do you know who I am Tom Carpenter?" Tom replied. "Well I don't know your name, but people say you are some kind of psychic that lives out in that field on the outer edge of town." The old woman nodded her head as she looked around for a minute. Then she looked at Tom and said. "My name is Evelyn Murray of Murray Manor and Estate. I'm not a psychic or a witch like people claim. I'm just old Tom Carpenter, and I'm tired from the walk. May I come in to rest for a bit?" Tom gave it a thought and said to the woman. "Alright... You can come inside to rest."

Tom held the door open while Evelyn stepped inside and he shut the door and began making his way back to the kitchen. On his way he asked the old woman. "Ms. Murray or is it Miss Murray?" The old woman grinned and said. "Just call me Evelyn if it's okay by you. Or by whatever makes you feel comfortable. I'm not picky." Tom replied, saying. "Evelyn it is then. You can call me Tom. You don't have to call me Tom Carpenter all the time." Evelyn looked him up and down and said. "Nope. You look like Tom Carpenter to me." Tom just shook his head and sat down at the table to finish his breakfast. Evelyn saw the other plate just sitting there so she sat down in front of it. Tom looked at her and quickly said. "Uh, that's for..." He paused and Evelyn was giving him a strange look. Then she asked him. "That's for who Tom Carpenter? I don't see anyone else here. Be a shame for such a fine meal to be wasted." Tom looked down for a moment and then back to Evelyn and said. "That's for you."

While the two of them were eating, Tom asked Evelyn. "What help did you think I needed?" Evelyn looked at Tom and said. "That coffee over there smells awful good." Tom nodded his head several times with a look of frustration, but he didn't say anything. Instead he got up and poured her a cup of coffee. Out of frustration, he didn't bother to even ask if she wanted milk and sugar with it even as he was looking at them. Tom walked over and sat the cup down beside Evelyn and he asked her. "Now will you answer my question?"

Evelyn took a sip of coffee, nodded her head in approval and said to Tom. "You make good coffee Tom Carpenter. Your wife said you made good coffee and she was right." Tom stopped eating and had a look of both curiosity and anger on his face as he asked. "You know my wife?" Evelyn replied. "I do." Tom leaned back in his chair for moment as the old woman finished eating. When she got nearly done, Tom asked her. "How do you know my wife?"

Evelyn took up the napkin and wiped her mouth as she too leaned back in her chair as she said to Tom. "You make a fine breakfast too Tom Carpenter, you surely do." Tom said to her. "Please. Tell me." Evelyn looked directly at Tom and said. "Your wife Kristi is the reason I am here Tom Carpenter, she is the reason for sure. She's lost you, and she asked me to help bring you to her." Tom now had a very confused look on his face and he asked. "What do you mean she lost me? I lost her! I got here from the hospital and she was gone. She's still gone!" Evelyn said to Tom. "In no way am I here to hurt you Tom Carpenter. No sir. Not in any way. She asked for my help and I'm trying to give it to her. But I can't help her unless I can help you. Tell me, Tom Carpenter; what happened to her? Do you remember?"

Tom lowered his head for a moment and he said to her. "I'm not really sure. I woke up here after my wreck and found condolence letters addressed to the Carpenter family. Since I am here and she is not, I can only assume she passed away somehow while I was in the hospital." Evelyn got a disgusted look on her face and she asked Tom. "You never checked? You never asked anyone where she was buried?" Tom stood up, put his coffee mug on the table and replied. "No. Now look. I'm not sure this is the right time or right kind of help I need so; thanks for stopping by but I can deal with this on my own."

Evelyn slowly got up out of her chair, looked Tom in the eyes and said. "Your wife said you would be hesitant to talk to me. She said you wouldn't be comfortable with this. It's okay Tom Carpenter. It's okay to be afraid of what you don't know, but at least take a chance at learning what you don't know." Tom said to her. "Well I know enough for now. I'm still willing to give you a ride home if you need it." Evelyn replied. "No need Tom Carpenter. I can walk. But if you like, I can show you how to find her. I can show you how to see her." Tom stood with his head down and he pointed his finger towards the door and said. "Please leave. Please just leave me be."

Tom was trying his hardest to be nice even as the disruption in his normal routine made him angry. Evelyn made her way to the door and as she opened it, she turned to Tom and said. "When you're ready Tom Carpenter, you can tell me about the wooden nickels your wife mentioned." Tom looked up quickly at the old woman with tears in his eyes and he kept pointing for her to leave.

Evelyn closed the door behind her as she left. Tom went into the kitchen and began his same routine of cleaning the dishes and wiping down the table. Afterwards he sat in his recliner like every other day, but saddened even more on this day. And just like the days before at dusk; Tom went into his daughter's room and hugged the skinny teddy bear. Just like the night before and the night before that one he covered his pillow with his wife's dirty shirt and laid in bed looking at the photo on the wall until he fell asleep. Tom couldn't help but think about everything the old woman had said, but he felt compelled to stay in that house. He felt that it where he belonged and that he must stay until his wife came home. But he couldn't help but wonder if his wife was in fact dead; and if so where was she buried?

Although Tom finished the day like so many others since his return from the hospital, the night didn't go the same way. During the night Tom's dreams were not like they were the many nights before. On this night, they were much more intense. For the first time in his dreams he heard his wife's voice call out to him, saying. "Come back to me Tom! Come back!"

Tom also dreamed about his daughter and the two wooden nickels. The flashes of light that Tom normally saw only once or twice in a night, he saw over and over on this particular night. With each flash of light, he could hear his wife calling out to him. Tom woke many times during the night; and each time he woke it became more fearful to fall back asleep. To Tom, sleep meant more bad dreams and deeper pain.

Sometime just before daylight and a little earlier than normal, Tom woke up and got up out of bed. He felt somewhat odd getting up earlier, but felt it was the best thing for him to do. Being that it was early Tom stood still in his bedroom at the foot of his bed for a spell trying to decide if he should start breakfast or wait till the normal time. Tom finally decided that he was being ridiculous, for he had never been such a creature of routine and habit before the wreck. So Tom went into the kitchen while still wearing his plain grey pajamas and white T-shirt to start the coffee.

He sat in his spot at the table while the coffee was making, and while sitting there a strange thought come across his mind. Tom whispered to himself. "There will be nine eggs in the egg carton and only three strips of bacon missing from the package; just like it was yesterday."

Tom got up quickly and went to the refrigerator to check his theory. He opened the stainless steel door of the refrigerator and then the egg carton. Like he thought; there were nine eggs in the carton. Tom grabbed the bacon package and looked it over real good to find only three strips were missing. At that point, his heart rate began to rise as he knew something was terribly wrong and he said to himself. "How's this possible?"

As Tom was getting ready to put the bacon back in the fridge, there was a knock at his front door. Tom hurried to the door hoping against all odds it would be his wife. He was still carrying the bacon in his left hand. When he opened the door, old lady Evelyn Murray was standing there leaning on a tall wooden staff and wearing the same old grey poncho. She quickly said to Tom. "If your wife is going to keep bothering me, I'm going to keep bothering you. Rather if you like it or not, so get used to it." Tom stood still, with a halfway grin on his face at her words, when he remembered he was still holding the bacon. Tom said to Evelyn. "Only three strips are missing."

Evelyn gave him a look with squinted eyes and her toothless jaws clenched together. Then she looked at the bacon and back to Tom and said. "Good.

There's enough for breakfast then. Now, may I come in or do I stand out here in the dark?" Tom shook his head as if he was coming out of a trance and he said to her. "Yes, by all means come in. Maybe you can make some sense of all this."

Once inside, Evelyn made her way to the table and sat down in the same spot she did the day before. Tom quickly made her a cup of coffee as if he were a young man hosting his parents for the first time. He handed her the cup and proceeded to pour his own. Evelyn took a sip of her coffee and said to Tom in a joking manner. "The only thing that doesn't make any sense is you not getting that bacon in the skillet." Tom looked down at the bacon, back to Evelyn, and said to her. "No, you don't understand. Every morning I cook the same amount of bacon and eggs, and every morning the same amount is there. Nine are eggs in the carton and only three strips of bacon gone. I haven't left to go grocery shopping. I should be out by now you see." Tom paused and gave Evelyn a good looking over and then he asked her. "Why are you carrying a staff? And why do you wear that old poncho all the time?"

Evelyn took a sip of coffee, looked at Tom with a smile and said. "Because it scares the crap out of those little shits that throw rocks at my house. I see them out by the road waiting on the school bus talking about my old house as if it's haunted. I know what they say about me. I was a kid once. That throwing rocks makes me so mad though. So, I found this old poncho in a resale shop for a dollar. The stick was dragged into my yard by a stray dog, but it seemed strong in case I needed to whack one of those little bastards. Only reason I'm wearing this old poncho and carrying the stick today is because they were out there waiting for the bus this morning. Made my day to sneak up and ramble some nonsense at them like I was casting a spell. Teach those little shits to mess with me."

When Evelyn got done speaking, she took a sip of coffee and winked at Tom with a smile of orneriness only an elderly person can acquire. For the first time in long time, Tom Carpenter smiled and chuckled a little while shaking his head at the old woman. Evelyn leaned back real quick, put her hand over her heart and said to Tom. "Dear God Tom Carpenter, you can smile. Be careful doing that. My ole ticker can't take too

22

many surprises." Tom shook his head again and said. "You're a mess Evelyn Murray." Evelyn replied. "Already told you; I'm old Tom Carpenter and I don't really give a damn what people think. No, I sure don't."

Tom looked down at the bacon sitting on the table and back to Evelyn. He wasn't quite sure how to put his next question to get an answer instead of an ornery remark from the old woman. Thankfully for him, she beat him to it by asking. "It's awful strange that you would ever notice. What have you done differently than you have been doing?"

Tom sat down with his cup of coffee and said while looking directly into Evelyn's eyes. "The only thing that's changed is you showed up. With that my dreams changed too." Evelyn asked. "What dreams Tom Carpenter? Tell me about them." Tom explained how his dreams normally played out and how they changed after Evelyn showed up. He explained to her about the flashes of light and being able to hear his wife call out to him. When he got done explaining it all to Evelyn, he asked her. "I think you know more than you're telling me so far? You said earlier that my wife was bothering you. My question is, given the bacon and eggs situation; and please tell me the truth. Am I dead?"

Evelyn grew a serious look on her face as she leaned forward in her chair and grasping her cup with both hands. She waited for just a moment for Tom's mind to clear of what he just said and she replied. "Dead as a doornail..." Tom had a look of disappointment and a little doubt on his face. Then Evelyn winked at him and said. "Physically, no you are not dead. Nor are you mentally dead.

Your soul is lost Tom Carpenter, and so is your wife's. You two are spiritually drifting through the astral plane clinging onto the things you recognize. She isn't lost as much as you, but she is still lost. I promised her I would try to reconnect you two." Tom sat with a confused look on his face and said to Evelyn. "I don't understand anything you just said."

Evelyn said back to Tom. "I know Tom Carpenter, I know. The astral plane is hard to understand and has many different doors and worlds. Its separates the land of living from those who are dead. It is a place only the soul can travel to. It is a place I must take you if you are to find your wife." Evelyn pointed the finger of her right hand at Tom and said. "You have to cross the plane Tom Carpenter. You have to cross the plane if you ever want to run out of eggs and bacon again."

Tom had a strange look on his face as he sat quietly for a moment. Evelyn never looked away but kept her eyes fixed on Tom. After several moments of what seemed to be a stare down, Tom said to her. "You know, an endless supply of bacon and eggs isn't all that bad." When Tom was done speaking, he held his cup up in the air as if he were making a toast. Evelyn lowered her head for a moment and then looked back at Tom and asked. "But is it worth the pain?"

At the sound of her words, Tom lowered his cup fast to rest it on the table as if it were extremely heavy and he said to her. "Nothing is worth the pain. I have to be with her." Evelyn grinned just a little and held her cup up in the air as to make a toast and she said to Tom. "Then we find her Tom Carpenter. We find her if you're willing to do what it takes." Tom leaned in and said with a low but serious voice. "I would do anything to see my Kristi again."

Upon hearing his words Evelyn squinted her eyes and it was obvious Tom's words struck a nerve. She whispered to herself. "My Kristi." Evelyn looked at Tom and said to him. "We can get started as soon as you cook those eggs and this bacon you got laying here. Unless that is, you're not in the mood for them like you have been every other day for so long." Tom stood silent looking down at the package of bacon on the table and after several moments passed; he picked it up and put it back in the refrigerator and said to Evelyn. "I don't believe you're hungry either." Evelyn smiled and said. "You'll do fine Tom Carpenter. You'll do fine."

CHAPTER 3

Tom asked Evelyn. "How do I cross the plane? This is all new to me. I still don't quite understand, and to be honest, I feel like I'm supposed to be here. I don't feel comfortable leaving." Evelyn said to Tom. "I know Tom Carpenter. I know you feel that way. What I know to be certain, your wife will never come through that door while you stay here. We must go to her."

Tom asked Evelyn. "Do you really have to call me by my first and last name? My mother use to call my dad whose name was also Tom Carpenter by his first and last name. It drove me crazy." Evelyn looked Tom over real good and said to him. "Everyone perceives things differently. To me you look like Tom Carpenter. I'm afraid at this point I wouldn't feel comfortable calling you Tom, or Mr. Carpenter."

Tom nodded his head and told the old woman he could learn to deal with it. Though Tom didn't tell Evelyn, there was something about her that made him feel like he had known her at some point in his life, but couldn't place it. Tom passed it off as just her personality starting to win him over to a new friendship. Tom refilled his cup with coffee and done the same for Evelyn. When he sat back down at the table, he noticed Evelyn's eyes were fixed on his cup stamped with #1 Dad. After a moment, Evelyn looked up at Tom with a sincere look and said. "I heard about your daughter some time back. I offer my condolences such as it is even though it is late."

Tom said to Evelyn. "Thank you. Late is fine too. It's more than my mother ever said about it." Evelyn asked Tom. "You and your mother don't get along? What happened Tom Carpenter that makes a man mad at his mother?" Tom quickly replied. "Another time Evelyn." The old woman didn't ask any more about his mother, but couldn't resist asking about his daughter when she said. "Your wife told me about two wooden nickels Tom Carpenter. Is it okay for me to ask about them?" Tom smiled a little for a moment and then his smile quickly turned to a frown but he said to her. "It's okay. It's a cute story between my daughter and me, but it has a sad ending Evelyn." The old woman took a sip of her coffee and said to Tom. "I know it does, but I want to hear it."

Tom took a deep breath, let it out slowly and said. "It started as kind of a joke when my daughter Amy was around four or five. Any time she would ask for a hug, I would reply. I only take wooden nickels. Meaning of course, something priceless also has no monetary value. Amy use to say to me that she didn't have any wooden nickels. So I would tell her she would have to owe me and I would give her a hug.

Well, my mother got wind of this and she had a solution, or a way to better the joke of it; depending on how you look at it. At the time, my mother reworked antique furniture to sell and she was good at it along with wood carving and toy making. She had gotten a chair that was quite wobbly as it had one leg that was a little shorter than the rest. So she cut a sliver off the bottom of three of the legs and from two of the slivers she made wooden nickels.

She secretly gave them to my daughter one evening while we were having dinner at her house, and it sure didn't take a minute for Amy to come asking for a hug. When I told her I only accept wooden nickels for hugs, her face lit up like a Christmas tree and she quickly pulled those nickels from her pocket and said to me. "I have two." Kristi and I were tickled and surprised. I knew instantly seeing the quality of woodwork that my mother was involved in it, but it was a good thing. From then on the nickels got passed back and forth as she and I would ask for a hug... When she died, I buried the wooden nickels with her knowing how much they meant to her."

Tom lowered his head after telling the story of the two wooden nickels and his lips tightened and jaws clenched several times. Evelyn could see that it hurt him to tell the story. She quickly diverted his attention by asking. "What happened to the third sliver cut from the bottom of the chair Tom Carpenter? What happened to it?" Tom kind of smiled and he said to Evelyn. "I never thought about it, but I guess she threw it away or done something with it. I don't really know."

Tom paused in deep thought and Evelyn sat quietly as he looked like he could say something at any time. After a minute of silence, Tom asked Evelyn. "Are you familiar with the smell of fresh rain Evelyn?" Evelyn replied. "Of course I am. Most people are." Tom looked around for a second and he went on to tell another story.

"When my daughter was alive, it always seemed to rain or storm when she made plans, or got excited to go do something. Now of course it didn't rain every time, but it was enough to notice. Eventually I started calling Amy, Storm Traveler. She didn't like it much but it was my little way of picking at her for always threatening to eat my fish in the pond." Tom paused again while he stared into his coffee cup and whispered to himself. "Storm Traveler." Tom looked at Evelyn and said. "I haven't been able to smell the rain, since she died. All these years later and I still can't smell a fresh summer rain. I don't guess I even remember exactly what it smelled like now."

Tom looked at Evelyn very seriously and sincere when he asked the old woman. "When are we going to look for my wife? When are you going to show me how to find her? Being without my daughter is hard enough on its own. I can't keep going on like this Evelyn. I need to find her." Evelyn slightly nodded her head several times and she said to Tom. "We are building the bridge Tom Carpenter. These stories, memories and emotions are what will lead us to her. I can show you how to cross the plane, but it's you who chooses where we go. If we could cross the plane while you're asleep and seeing the flashes of light while hearing her voice; it would be easy. It just doesn't work that way Tom Carpenter, no it doesn't. We have to do it the hard way, but we need a bridge in the right direction."

Tom said to Evelyn. "You know more about this stuff than I do, but understand it's not easy talking about all this." Evelyn squinted her eyes at him and said. "It's not easy for me to be here either. No it isn't. My granddaughter is in the hospital as we speak. She's very ill Tom Carpenter, and I am here with you." Tom stood silent for a moment with a confused look upon his face, and then he asked Evelyn. "Who is your granddaughter?" Evelyn replied. Her name is Ashley.

I believe she use to come by here and feed your fish." Tom grew a saddened look and said. "I sure liked that little girl. She's sweet as she can be. So why are you here instead of there with her?" Evelyn replied. "There is nothing I can do for her Tom Carpenter; nothing at all. You on the other hand, I can do something for you."

Tom went on to explain to Evelyn how he understood how hard it is to have a child hurt and no way to help. He thanked the old woman for being willing to try to help him when she had troubles of her own. Out of curiosity, Tom asked Evelyn. "How is it that you come to be the one to take care of your granddaughter?" Evelyn sat down at the table and said to Tom. "You better sit down Tom Carpenter." Tom sat down and Evelyn said to him. "What I'm about to say is going to bother you deeply, but you can't let it take your attention away from your wife." Tom nodded his head and assured Evelyn he would stay focused.

Evelyn's eyes wondered about for a moment and she said to Tom. "My son Draven was out drinking with some friends of his when my granddaughter was still little. He decided to drive home one morning when he shouldn't have. He fell asleep at the wheel and hit a young girl head on, killing her. My granddaughter Ashley was only six years old when it happened. She's fourteen now. Her dad has been in prison most of her life because of that wreck he caused. He lost his chance at being a father to her, and now it looks very possible he will never have the chance."

Tom had a heavy frown on his now red face from the rise of his blood pressure. He said to Evelyn. "You say the wreck happened about seven and a half years ago? 1992 Maybe?" Evelyn sighed heavily and lowered her head for a moment. Then she raised her eyes to Tom and said. "You are correct Tom Carpenter. It was my son who killed your Amy." Tom stood up, staggered a little and said to Evelyn while pointing his finger to the door once more. "You don't owe me Evelyn, but I don't think you can help me. Please leave me be."

Tom started to his bedroom, but staggered like a drunk as he fought off fainting in the floor. Evelyn got up and went to help Tom what little she could and she said to him. "Let me help you get to bed, then I'll show myself out." Tom was too weak to argue and had little choice but to let her help him. When they got to the bed in Tom's room he let go of Evelyn, fell on the bed and rolled over on his back with his feet still on the floor. Tom's breathing was fast and Evelyn stayed still standing beside him for moment to see if he would be okay. Tom put his hands over his face and began rubbing his eyes when he heard Evelyn take a quick gasp of air. He peeked through his fingers and saw her with her hands over her mouth and starring toward the pillows. Tom knew what she was looking at.

Evelyn asked with a sound of complete surprise, excitement and concern in her voice. "What is this Tom Carpenter!? Is this your wife's shirt around your pillow?" Tom replied with his hands still over his face. "I know it's silly. I do. But it helps me feel close to her." Evelyn slowly picked up the pillow with her eyes fixed on it and she said to Tom. This is not silly Tom Carpenter. No it isn't. This is powerful. Yes, very powerful this is." She walked around to stand at Tom's feet while still holding the pillow and she said to Tom. You called her, my Kristi and you have her shirt around your pillow." Tom said to her. "Yes I do call her that. Yes I have her shirt wrapped around my pillow. I told you it's silly. Can we drop it now?"

Evelyn laid the pillow down on the bed next to Tom and said. "Your wife calls you, my Tommy when you're not with her.

Did you know that Tom?" Tom replied. "No I didn't know that." Evelyn said to him. "That's not all Tom Carpenter, that's not all. She also wraps one your worn shirts around her pillow when you are gone. She does this every night while she waits for you. Do you understand what this means?" Tom moved his hands, sat up and replied. "No I do not."

Evelyn looked at the pillow and then back to Tom and she said to him. "You and Kristi are doing the same thing to connect with each other without knowing it. You're soul mates Tom Carpenter. You hear me, you're soul mates. Oh this changes things, this surely does. I never actually believed it existed until now... Soul mates." Tom asked. "I knew she was from the moment I first saw her. Tell me Evelyn Murray; how does this change anything?" Evelyn replied. "Because now we are running out of time."

CHAPTER 4

Tom stood up and walked around his room for a moment as his mind wondered. Evelyn eventually asked him? "Are you okay?" Tom stopped walking, turned to Evelyn and said in frustration. "I don't know Evelyn, your guess is as good as mine." Tom ran his fingers through his hair and he said to Evelyn. "I need some coffee. You want some?" Evelyn asked. "You don't want me to leave now Tom Carpenter?" Tom replied. "Call it entertaining my curiosity, but I rather you stay."

Tom and Evelyn went back to the kitchen. Evelyn sat down at the table and Tom poured them both a cup of coffee. When Tom sat down he asked Evelyn. "Did you ever tell Kristi about your son and what he did?" Evelyn took a sip of her coffee and she said to Tom. "Yes I did Tom Carpenter, I surely did. Like you, it was hard for her too. She was willing to move past it Tom Carpenter to try and be with you. Now are you willing to move past it to be with your Kristi?"

Tom said to Evelyn. "I'm not mad at you Evelyn. Please understand that. This is all just a lot to take in at one time. But yes, I am willing to do whatever it takes to be with my wife." Tom looked directly in Evelyn's eyes and said. "Why are we running out of time? How does being soul mates change anything?"

Evelyn said to Tom. "Soul mates don't just die in physical form Tom Carpenter. If they don't connect in the afterlife their souls refuse to live. If we don't find her, you will die Tom Carpenter and there will be no crossing over. You will be gone both physically and spiritually. Likewise; Kristi will perish without you." Tom said to her. "I have no choice but to believe you. And the reason I do believe you is; I can't keep going without her. I know it. I can feel it Evelyn. I can feel myself coming to an end. So help me if you can. Let's get this going Evelyn."

Evelyn grinned a little and said to Tom. "We already have Tom Carpenter, we already have. But the thoughts of your daughter have clouded your mind. I need you to focus on your wife. Tell me how you met her. Tell me how you and Kristi met." It became instantly obvious that Tom thought about how he and Kristi had met. His eyes lit up and for the first time in a long time. He had a peaceful look on his face along with a smile.

When he smiled, Evelyn said to him. "Christ! Tom Carpenter you really should warn someone before you smile. It's a nice smile don't get me wrong; but I'm just not use to seeing it." Tom took a sip of his coffee and whispered his wife's name to himself while still smiling. He looked up at Evelyn and said to her. "We met at a carwash one evening. She was in the bay next to mine washing her car. What caused us to meet was the wall between us didn't go to the ceiling.

Every time I would spray the top of my truck, she was getting sprayed on the other side. Eventually I guess she got tired of it. She came around the front and yelled to get my attention, and get my attention she did. She looked so beautiful to me standing there in the light of the evening sun. She was wearing a plane light blue v-cut t-shirt, and tight blue jeans. Her hair and shirt were slightly wet and she looked mad, which of course made her look even more intoxicating to me. So I let go of the trigger to see what she wanted.

She explained that I was getting her wet by spraying over the wall. I apologized but when she turned around I sprayed her ankles, getting her black heeled boots wet. She called me an ass and walked on to the other side. I laughed a little but didn't think much else about it. I just started back to washing my truck when I felt the water hit my back. I knew who it was. When I turned around she had one hand over her mouth as she was laughing at me and that's when the water fight began. When the time ran out on the counter; I offered to replace her clothes. She told me I was being ridiculous, but suggested I buy her dinner instead... I never told her or anyone for that matter, but I fell in love with her when the water hit my back. I knew then, if she was that ornery I had to be with her."

Evelyn had a smile on her face as she listened to Tom's story and when he was done she said to him. "We'll find her Tom Carpenter, that we will. I hope you understand this won't be as easy as just crossing the plane and it's done. There's work to do here before the end." Tom assured Evelyn that he was ready to do whatever it took, and face whatever he had to in order to be with his wife.

Evelyn looked at Tom with a questioning look, then nodded her head and asked Tom for a large pan or a bowl big enough his feet would fit inside. Tom gave the old woman a strange look but didn't ask any questions. He got up and dug around in the walnut stained oak cabinets until he found a turkey pan. When he showed it to Evelyn, she told him that it would work fine and that he might want to add some lukewarm water to it.

Tom asked Evelyn. "Why do I need water in the pan and why am I going to put my feet in it?" Evelyn replied. "Water lubricates the transition. It would also keep you from burning alive if we wind up in the wrong place across the plane." Tom looked at Evelyn with a serious look and asked. "Are you suggesting we could end up in Hell?" Evelyn grew a very serious look on her face and said to Tom. "It is possible though extremely rare. It's not something you need to be too worried about Tom Carpenter."

Tom nodded his head and asked. "Okay, but how is that even possible?" Evelyn replied. "The doors to Hell are always open. The doors to Heaven only open by invite. You won't wind up in Heaven for sure Tom Carpenter. At least not on this journey." Tom laughed a little and said to Evelyn. "Well I'm glad you cleared that up Evelyn. I kind of felt doomed there for a minute." Evelyn smiled and said to Tom. "I do apologize for making you feel doomed Tom Carpenter. Now sit that pan on the floor in front of your chair and let's get started."

Tom sat the pan down in front of his chair and he took a seat. While taking his shoes and socks off, Evelyn saw the nervousness in his eyes and she said to him. "Try to relax Tom Carpenter. It's not going to hurt." Tom nodded his head but the nervousness was still noticeably present. Evelyn got up without saying a word and went into Tom's bedroom. Tom didn't say anything but stopped what he was doing for a moment and he watched to see what she was up to. Evelyn had taken Kristi's shirt off of Tom's pillow and she brought into the kitchen and gave it to Tom and asked. "You would do anything, yes?" Tom replied. "Anything." Evelyn scooted her chair closer to Tom's. Then she sat down and said to him. "Then let's go find your Kristi."

Evelyn reached out and patted the top of Tom's hand that was resting on the table and she said to him. "Just relax. Now rest your hands in your lap and close your eyes." Tom done what he was told and Evelyn continued. "Take a deep breath and let it out slowly while casting out all of your thoughts. Only focus on the black you see behind your eyes lids. Just focus on the nothing of what you see." Evelyn closed her eyes and let out a slow breath and then she said to Tom. "Now see, but not imagine yourself standing up and looking at yourself sitting in that chair."

Evelyn didn't say anything out loud, even as her lips were still moving. She had crossed into the astral plane but Tom had not. This went on for several minutes and Tom said to Evelyn in frustration. "I can't do it! I can't see anything! I'm just sitting here playing make believe. It's not going to work on me Evelyn. I'm sorry."

CHAPTER 5

Evelyn slowly opened her eyes and she had an almost furious look on her face. She said to Tom. "I won't let you be sorry Tom Carpenter." As soon as she said those words, she sprung out of her chair extremely fast and wrapped her hands around Tom's neck. Evelyn tightened her grip and Tom's eyes grew wide as he couldn't believe the old woman was trying to choke him.

Tom reached up and grabbed her hands to pull them away but he couldn't. Tom pulled and couldn't believe how strong the old woman was. Tom looked at Evelyn in surprise and he fought harder to pull her hands away. Evelyn said to him with a straining voice as she kept choking him. "I'm not going to kill you! You have to trust me! I'm doing this for you!"

Tom couldn't help but pull at her arms and even try to hit her, it was a natural response. Even as he fought

Evelyn's grip her words, "I'm doing this for you" rang like bells in his head. It was what his mother use to say to him when they argued over her crossing the plane to see his father.

Just as Tom was about to pass out he heard Evelyn say. "The lonely light pole at the end of town… Take us there."
At the end of the street that ran beside Tom's house and at the far end of the town limits stood a lonely black light pole. It was put there to shed light on a metal bench that use to be the stop for the town. There were no houses around that end of town as it was all forest and private land. Even though the city built a new bus stop, they kept the light on over the old rusty bench for historical purposes. It was always a good place to meet, but it wasn't where Tom and Evelyn ended up. Just as Tom's eyes faded shut for a moment, he heard Evelyn's voice say to him. "Open your eyes Tom." Tom opened his eyes expecting to be sitting in his chair beside his kitchen table, but where he was deeply surprised both him and Evelyn.

Tom and Evelyn were standing in the front yard of an older single story brick home that had an attached carport and small metal building beside the house. Evelyn asked Tom. "Where have you brought us Tom?" He turned to Evelyn and said. "So now you call me Tom instead of Tom Carpenter." Evelyn said to him. "Now you look like Tom, maybe even Tommy, but not Tom Carpenter." Tom said to her. "Please don't call me Tommy. My mother use to call me that. It's not even my name. It's just plane Tom." Evelyn nodded her head and asked. "Okay, so where are we?" Tom replied. "We are at my mother's house."

Evelyn asked. "Why have you brought us here?" Tom replied. "When you said you were doing this for me, it made me think of her. I guess that's why." Tom looked around for a minute and said. "I haven't been here in a long time. It doesn't appear to have changed at all." Evelyn said to him. "You are across the plane now Tom. Nothing here is like it is in the world you know. Even people can take a different appearance. Very little of anything here is actually as it seems… Now tell me Tom. What is your mother's name?"

Tom looked at Evelyn and said. "Her name is Katie." Evelyn asked. "I take it you haven't seen her in a long time." Tom replied. "No I haven't. Not since right after my daughter died."

Tom looked around again and began walking towards the house. Evelyn followed him but didn't say anything else. When Tom got to the old barn red door of the house, he opened it without knocking or announcing his arrival. Evelyn gave him a strange look and said. "You just walk into houses unannounced do you?" Tom smiled and said as his eyes wondered. "I don't think she's here." Evelyn put her hand on Tom's shoulder and when he turned to her, she said to him. "You might be surprised Tom."

Tom asked. "What is it you're not telling me?" As he asked, something caught his attention that seemed more important than the answer he wanted from Evelyn. Tom walked over to a beautifully crafted and hand carved maple desk and he put his hands on the back of an old wooden four legged chair. He turned to Evelyn and said. "I can't believe she kept this thing. It's the chair she cut the slivers from to make the wooden nickels." Tom looked around at the whole living area and he said to Evelyn. "She made everything in here except for this chair."

The living area had many pieces of furniture made from unique pieces of wood. Even the couch was carved from a single piece of large tree trunk and the front of both arm rest had the face of what appeared to be a wizard carved in them. There were two matching oak rocking chairs carved to look like they were a pair of snakes with the mouths open at the hand rest. Each piece was unique and well-designed. The floor of the living area was made from butcher block squares and specifically placed by color to create a globe and compass.

Tom took a good look around the room and said. "She sure is talented… It's too bad she went crazy." He looked over at Evelyn and she was leaned against the wall by the door looking at Tom. She also had a look as if she had seen all these things before. Tom noticed it and Evelyn knew he did. She said to him. "I knew your mother Tom. I think you've figured that much out by now." Tom said while his head was lowered and rubbing his fingers across the top of the chair. "I suspected it. If I'm right, she started coming to see you after my dad passed away."

Evelyn nodded her head to let Tom know he was right. Then she asked him. "What happened between you and your mother Tom?" Tom replied. "I don't really want to get into it if that's okay." Evelyn shook her head and said to him. "Take a look around Tom. We are deep into it. You are going to have to get passed this if we are to move on. Now tell me, what happened between you and your mother."

Tom took a seat in the chair he had been standing by. Evelyn walked over and sat in a heavily padded chair that was made from woven vines. Tom said to Evelyn. "That was her favorite chair and one of her first to make like that. It's also where she was sitting when we got the news my dad had a heart attack at work and passed away.

I was a boy then. Just twelve years old when that happened. It was a hard time for us going through that alone. She and I stayed close for a while but it didn't last. She started having dreams about dad. I don't think she could realize at the time, it was only dreams. I think she believed it was all real. She sure acted as if those dreams were real. It was like they become memories of a time she never got to live. It was very strange."

Tom paused for a moment as he remembered more and more. Evelyn said to him in a calm voice. "Go on Tom. Tell the rest of it." Tom gave her a quick look but his eyes returned to the floor as he went on to say. "She only had the dreams about dad a few times, but it was enough to drive her mad.

She started buying and reading books on spirituality, realms and different stuff along those lines. It didn't bother me until she started practicing that stuff. I thought it was some kind of witchcraft and that she was trying to bring dad back and that's what really bothered me.

I remember getting into a bad argument with her one night when I was in my later teens. I finally told her to leave him alone. Let dad rest, I said to her. She stood right in the middle of this room with a confused look on her face and arms out to the side and said to me. "I'm doing this for you Tommy."

Tom looked at Evelyn as he slightly nodded his head. She knew he was referring to her words when she was choking him. It was his explanation of what brought the two of them to where they were at this point.

Tom went on and said. "I couldn't believe she was going to use me as the reason for her going crazy. I didn't want to be her excuse, so I left. I stayed with a friend till school was over. Then like most boys out of school, I went to work so I could get my own place. I guess the rest is history from there."

Evelyn cocked her head to the side a little with a grin and said to Tom. "Oh Tom, I don't think that's the end. If she made two wooden nickels for you knowing what you and your daughter had going on with the hugs; you must have reconciled at some point. Didn't you?"

Tom explained, saying. "Well yes we did reconcile when she found out I was going to get married. And for a long while she didn't do or say anything crazy. She was a huge help to Kristi and me with Amy when she was little. Every now and then she would say something a little off but not much. That is until Amy passed away.

My mother came to the house to try and comfort Kristi and me by saying she could show us how to see Amy again. She said it doesn't have to be the end just because she died. It made Kristi and me furious. We just needed time to heal and move on, but my mother kept pushing the issue. It was as if she wanted us to join her craziness. So we finally told her to leave and not to come back."

Evelyn said to Tom. "And here you are doing what you hated her for asking you to do." Tom quickly looked at Evelyn and said. "I didn't abandon my child to do this." Tom's words angered Evelyn. She stood up, pointed her finger at him and said. "Don't you think for one minute she abandoned you. I remember well what she went through. Like most people in that town she thought I was a witch of some kind. She came to see me just like your wife done a short time ago.

Your mother came to see what I knew. And all your mother could talk about was what your father said to her in those dreams and how she needed to be ready to help you when the time came. So don't give me that story Tom Carpenter. You may believe it's true but it isn't... Now, do you want to know what your father said to her Tom? Or do you know already?"

Tom sat motionless for a moment just staring at Evelyn as he tried to remember. He finally said to her. "No I don't guess so." Evelyn walked over close to Tom and said. "He told her she would have to help Hammerhead when he needed it most but least expected it. Hammerhead as he called you would one day have to cross the plane to save his own soul." Tom smiled for a minute and said to himself. "Hammerhead." Then he looked at Evelyn and said. "That's what he used to call me when I was little because I always bumped my head into stuff." Tom whispered the word to himself as he self-indulged in the memories of being little with his father. "Hammerhead."

Then Tom looked back to Evelyn and said. "So she done all that to help me cross over and complete this quest huh? Oh wait, she's not here is she?" Evelyn said to him. "Don't be so hard on her Tom. Just because you don't see her doesn't mean she isn't here. I got to know her well, and I can say with certainty that she is always there for you. Even if you can't see or believe it."

Tom replied. "The only one I see here is you." Evelyn said to him. "I wouldn't be here if not for your mother. If not for Katie Carpenter, I wouldn't have given your wife the time of day. I knew you before this happened, and I knew this day would come. I am helping you because your mother never gave up. Her determination earned my respect Tom."

Tom said to Evelyn. "Let me show you something." Evelyn nodded her head and Tom opened the top right drawer of the desk and reached inside. He pulled out a circular piece of wood around twelve inches in diameter. When Tom turned it over to show it to Evelyn, she quickly saw it was an engraved portrait of Tom's family.

His portrait along with his wife Kristi's were obvious. Those two were as clear as a photo. However; the girl in the portrait didn't quite look like Tom's daughter Amy. Tom's daughter had higher cheekbones, deeper eye sockets and a pointier chin. The girl in the engraved portrait had a round face and chin, but not so round as to suggest she was overweight, and her eye sockets were shallow. She was still a pretty girl based on the portrait, but definitely not Amy.

Tom said to Evelyn. "My mother is extremely good at engraving portraits of people. She would never have made this kind of mistake. I don't know who she had in mind here. It kind of looks like the little girl who likes to feed my fish, but it's clearly not my daughter.

She made this right after my daughter passed away, and she tried to give it to me. Well it just made things worse. It hurt Kristi terribly to see it as well. Maybe you have to face the fact that she was a little crazy." Evelyn took the portrait from Tom and she grew a very sad look on her face. As she looked at it, she rubbed her fingers over the face of the girl in the portrait and said to Tom. "You are correct in one thing Tom. This is not your daughter.

This is my granddaughter Ashley." Tom asked. "Why would your granddaughter be in a portrait with my wife and me?" Evelyn replied. "That remains to be discovered, doesn't it Tom?" Tom said to her as he took back the wooden portrait to put it back in the desk. "Yes it does."

Once Tom put the portrait back, he leaned up and something caught his eye at the far window of the living area. He looked and shouted in surprise and fear. "Christ! Look!" He said to Evelyn. She turned and saw what he was looking at.

There were people standing at that window and every other window of the house. Multiple people were standing at each window and they covered the yard area as well. Tom stood still watching them as he grew fearful of why they would be there. Evelyn quickly said to him. "We have to go Tom! We have to go now!"

Tom asked with a both excited and fearful voice. "What do they want?" Evelyn looked at Tom and said. "They know you're not dead Tom. They want you to take them back to the land of the living. They want to claim your body as their own while you stay here... We have to go Tom!" Tom said loudly as he watched the windows. "I don't know how Evelyn!"

The old woman walked over and took Toms right hand in her left hand and she said to him. "Close your eyes Tom and focus on the lonely light pole." Tom replied. "I don't think I want to close my eyes Evelyn." Tom was focused on the people standing all around outside and didn't want to take his eyes off of them.

Evelyn said to him. "You have to if we're going to get out of here." At that moment Tom realized how much he had grown to trust the old woman, because he was willing to give it a try. Tom closed his eyes, and after a brief moment he smiled and said. "I see it." Evelyn said to him.

"Watch out for the tree limb that hangs outward beside it." She was referring to an elm limb that hangs out into the road beside the bench. Anyone who drives through there gets there vehicle wacked or themselves if they're not watching. Tom said loudly. "I see the limb." Evelyn quickly told him to duck the limb and at the same time she slapped him hard across the face.

CHAPTER 6

Tom put his left hand on his face as he leaned over and shouted from the sting of the slap. "Damn it! I thought I ducked it!" When he opened his eyes, he stood up straight seeing the light pole and said. "We made it." Tom looked to his left and there was nothing but the old dirt road and forest on both sides. The light pole and old rusty bench were in front of him.

When Tom looked to his right he was surprised to see a different woman than Evelyn standing next to him. This woman was in her mid-forties with a slim build and nice figure. She had sandy blonde hair and was wearing blue jeans, a blue and white checkered shirt and heeled boots.

Tom quickly asked the woman. "Who are you?" The woman replied in a smooth and fluent voice; rather than the old raspy voice with a southern draw she did before. "It's me Tom Carpenter. It's me Ms. Evelyn Murray." Tom looked her over real good and he said to her. "I don't think so... Evelyn never went by the name Ms..."

Evelyn said to him. "I told you before; people sometimes look different across the plane. Here in this part of it; this is who and how I see myself. Just like you now look like Tom Carpenter to me instead of just Tom... Anyway; just so you know, you did duck the limb. It was me that wacked you Tom Carpenter, it was me."

Tom rubbed his face a little more and asked as he was slightly angered by the revelation. "Well what the hell did you do that for!?" Evelyn said to him. "I wanted to make sure you focused on this spot instead of what you were seeing in the windows. We don't have time Tom Carpenter, to end up somewhere we shouldn't be. We still have work to do. Got some unfinished business to tend to."

Tom gave her a both angered and confused look as he said to her. "You're some piece of work, you know that! I thought you were here to help, and end up beating the shit out of a guy. Kind of think you might have done that for sport. "Evelyn stood there in the appearance of a middle aged blonde woman with her hands on her hips listening to Tom as he complained.

When he was done, she held her hands out to her sides and asked. "Are you done whining now? You'll live Tom Carpenter and we are where we need to be. So if you're done, let's move on. It could be a long walk unless we get lucky."

Tom shook his head at her and replied. "Well let's get going then." Evelyn started to head in the direction of the dirt road away from town. But after only a few steps she stopped and held her hand out motioned for Tom to stop as well. Tom asked. "What is it?" Evelyn turned to Tom, pulled back her long blonde hair and said. "I know this place... Do you know where we are Tom Carpenter?" Tom just shook his head no as he looked around very carefully and suspiciously. Evelyn said to him. "We are in purgatory. Though I'm not sure why. This place is dangerous Tom Carpenter and has many doorways. You don't want to get lost here for sure. No you don't."

Tom asked while pointing his finger at the light pole. "Then why did you want me to bring us here?" Evelyn looked at the light pole and then all around the area. There was no one else there besides the two of them. After a brief moment of silence, she said to him. "Someone very powerful is in this place; someone very powerful indeed. Whoever this person may be; they are a missing piece of the puzzle Tom Carpenter. This is a piece of the puzzle we must have before you can move on."

Tom asked. "What puzzle? What are you talking about now?" Evelyn turned to Tom with her hair covering the right side of her face. She glared at Tom with a pause before she said. "We are putting back all the pieces that are part of you. It would seem Tom Carpenter, for you to be at peace enough to focus only on your wife; we must first find the other lost parts of your soul. Some parts get hurt so deeply they are cast away. It's those little pieces that never let a soul rest. It is the unfinished business that prevents the crossing Tom Carpenter." Evelyn looked around for a moment with her hands on her hips and then she said while looking down the dirt road past the pole. "Ah, it's this way."

Tom held his hands out to his sides, laughed and said to her. "That's the way we were going to go to start with." Evelyn replied as she started walking past the light pole and Tom. "No. It wasn't this way when we got here. You can get lost very easily here Tom Carpenter. Luckily for us, it's the right way now."

Tom shook his head again and hurried to catch up and walk beside Evelyn. The two of them walked for a while down the old dark dirt road without saying much to each other. Only the sounds of the gravel moving under their feet, and Tom's racing heart broke the silence. That is, until a light in the distance caught Tom's attention.

He pointed to it and said to Evelyn. "I don't remember a light being down here along the road. There is only one, that I know for sure. All the houses on this road are back in the woods down long driveways." Evelyn said to him. "That is not a light from a house. It's a light from a light pole like the one we started at." Tom said to her. " I just said there are no more light poles on this road." Evelyn laughed and said. "Here in purgatory, there may be thousands that all look the same. However; Tom Carpenter I have a feeling we may get lucky and this be the one we're looking for."

As they got closer to the light Tom and Evelyn could see a man standing next to a bench. The man swayed back and forth as he laughed about something. As Tom and Evelyn got a little closer they could also a girl lying down on the bench. The man standing next to her was telling stories and holding something in his hand.

Tom and Evelyn kept walking towards the man and girl and soon were able to hear the man say the word "sasquatch" as he told a story and then broke out in laughter again. Tom whispered to Evelyn. "My dad use to talk about sasquatch, bigfoot or whatever you want to call it." Evelyn didn't say anything, nor did she even acknowledge what Tom had said. She just kept walking with a serious almost saddened look on her face.

Evelyn not responding to Tom along with the look on her face made Tom even more nervous. He felt nervous approaching the other people and Evelyn's behavior heightened his anxiety about it.

As Tom and Evelyn got close, the man spotted them and stopped talking and laughing. He just stood still and watched them approach. The girl looked up just for a second with her hair covering most of her face but quickly laid back down as if she didn't care who it was. Tom couldn't see much of the girl lying on the bench as her brunette hair had her face covered. She was wearing a dark blue jacket, very light faded colored pants and white running shoes. No more than Tom could see, there was no way to know who she could have been.

Tom moved his attention to the man standing beside the bench and gave him a good looking over in case there was trouble. The man was about five foot ten inches tall, slim build with natural light tan. He had a close trimmed mustache light brown hair that part of hanged down in front of his forehead with the rest of it combed back. It was surely the hairstyle of a man with a good buzz or completely drunk. The man was wearing black cowboy boots, faded blue jeans with slight tears above the knees and a white tank top undershirt. In his right hand he held a can of beer and a cigarette in the other.

The man didn't pay much attention to Tom other than a quick look, smile and nod. He seemed fixed on Evelyn and it was noticeable. In her chosen appearance of the blonde, well-built middle aged woman is was easy to see why a man like this one who appeared to be around the same age, would be eyeing her. Evelyn said to the man as if she had known him for many years. "Hello John."

It was easy for Tom to see that Evelyn cared for this man as if they were very close friends of the past. The man said back to Evelyn. "It's been a long time." Then the man paused, Evelyn gave him a quick smile and said. "Too long." Tom said to the both of them. " Well you two obviously know each other." Evelyn looked at Tom with a smile on her face and said. "John and I go way back. We were friends in another life and time." The man said to Tom. "I'm John Raeburn. People around here just call me J.R..." Tom said to the man. "Well if you're a friend of Evelyn's I'm glad to meet you."

Tom was about to introduce himself but Evelyn interrupted him by moving unusually close to him as she said. "John. This is my good friend, Tom Carpenter." When Evelyn said his name, the girl on the bench sat up extremely fast with her hair still covering her face she called out with loud voice. "Daddy!" Then the girl quickly pulled back her hair and for the first time in years, both she and Tom were looking at each other.

Tom gasps, took a step back and began to tremble all over. Evelyn knew what was going to happen as to why she moved so close to Tom. She quickly grabbed Tom under his right elbow with her right hand and had her left hand on his back to help stabilize him. Evelyn was saying to him at the same time she held him up. "It's okay Tom."

John rushed over as well and held Tom from the other side. Tom never moved his eyes from Amy's face even as he wilted to his knees. Amy smiled said in low almost whispering voice. "My daddy." Then she smiled and started to cry at the same time as she rushed over to throw her arms around Tom's neck.

When Amy hugged Tom he was motionless for a second or two until the familiar smell of her hair hit him. At that moment, it became real. Tom closed his eyes and wrapped both his arms around her and cried out as his body trembled. "Oh my God!" Tom was a strong man and done well not to break down and sob like a baby. But Tom Carpenter was all heart for his family and nothing can hurt a man like their children can. Tom couldn't hold back his tears of joy as they ran down his cheeks.

However; seeing Amy once again broke his heart all over again. Amy also done well not to sob as her heart broke as well. Like her dad, the tears of both joy and sadness flowed down her cheeks. The two of them were overcome with the joy of seeing each other, and at the same time grief struck by the realization the visit would be short lived.

Amy leaned back and Tom put his hands on the sides of her head to pull her in so he could kiss the top her head. As he kissed her, Amy said to him. "I can't believe you're here dad." Tom leaned back to look at his daughter one more time as he just couldn't believe it was actually her and not a trick. When she smiled at him, he pulled her back in and wrapped his arms back around her and said. "My sweet baby girl... Still hugging her Tom continued. "I can't believe it's really you sweetie." Tom took one deep breath after another through his gritted teeth as he desperately tried not to break down.

Amy leaned back, looked her dad in the eyes and asked. "Why are you here dad?" Tom ran his hand down Amy's head, shoulder and arm to grab her hand as he said. "I had to see you Sweetie." Tom gritted his teeth even tighter while taking short fast breaths and said. "I had to find you." Amy put a hand on each of Tom's shoulders and said to him. "I'm so happy you did. I've missed you so much." Still trying to get his emotions under control, Tom replied. "Oh sweetie; I can't explain how much I've missed you." Tom wiped his eyes and nose, looked at Amy and said. "Every night I go to your room and give skinny a hug for you." Amy smiled and replied with a whispering voice. "Skinny."

Suddenly Amy's eyes got a little wider and she leaned up a little, reached into her right front pocket and said to Tom. "I haven't forgotten daddy. Let me pay for the hug." Amy pulled her hand out of her pocket and said to Tom. "Hold out your hands dad, you know." Tom gritted his teeth so hard the grinding could be heard by the other two standing close by. He was a proud man and like most men, he didn't want his daughter of all people to see him cry.

Tom held out his trembling hands cupped together as if he were getting a drink from a stream; knowing at the same time what Amy was about to give him. Amy reached out and put the two wooden nickels in her dad's hands. For Tom Carpenter it was too much to bear.

Upon seeing the wooden nickels in his hands; the memory of the last time he saw them rushed back. It was a flash in

Tom's mind of him putting the two wooden nickels in Amy's coffin as he whispered to her lifeless body. "Keep them till I join you sweetie." At that moment a man among men who carried himself as a proud independent strong man, lost all control of his power and emotion. Tom held the wooden nickels to his face as he leaned over with his knees and head on the ground. He had broken.

It was hard for Evelyn and John to watch such a man break so hard. Tom was all heart for his girls. His love for them was his power, strength and it was his love that made him the man he was.

John and Evelyn eventually just looked at each other as it was too hard to watch Tom leaned over like he was. Amy however stayed right with him. She leaned on his back with her arms around him, telling him it was okay. She repeated several times. "It's okay daddy. It's okay. I'm right here."

After several moments Tom gathered his composure and sat up. He wiped his nose and eyes again with a handkerchief and said to Amy. "I'm sorry Amy. I just missed you so much sweetie." Amy replied. "I missed you too dad. I missed you and mom." Amy got a confused look on her face and she asked. "Where is mom? How is she?" Evelyn stepped in and said. "Your mother is okay Amy." Amy looked back to her dad and said. "Dad?" Tom stood up with Amy standing with him and she asked. "What's going on dad? Is she?" Again, Evelyn spoke up. "No Amy. Your mother isn't dead. Your mom and dad are lost souls right now trying to find each other." Amy asked Evelyn. "You're helping them, right?" Evelyn replied. "Yes I am Amy."

Tom looked at Evelyn and back to say to Amy. "Evelyn has helped me this far and I found you sweetie." Amy got a strange look on her face and asked. "You call her Evelyn. Why?" Tom looked over at Evelyn and figured it was the different appearance that had Amy confused. Tom said to her. "That's her name sweetie." Amy looked at Evelyn who winked at her without Tom seeing it. Amy said to her dad. "Okay. I didn't recognize her."

CHAPTER 7

Tom and Amy took a seat on the bench beside each other while Evelyn and John stood back talking among themselves. Amy asked Tom. "How did you and mom get separated?" Tom replied. "I'm not quite sure sweetie. I had a wreck myself and don't remember much after it. I woke up at home and your mother wasn't there. I don't know what happened to her." Amy put her hand on Tom's shoulder and said to him. "Find her dad." Tom replied with a slight grin. "I'm going to try baby girl." Tom gave Amy another hug and then said to her. "First I have to figure out how to get you out of here."

Tom's words caught Amy off guard as well as John and Evelyn. Amy gave her dad a strange look and said to him. "I belong here dad. I can't leave." Tom didn't quite understand what that meant but there was no way he was willing to leave her after just finding her. Tom looked over at Evelyn and John for a moment to see what they might have to say.

John popped the top on a new can of beer, looked around and said referring to the beer. "Well, last Mohican right here." Amy laughed a little and said to Tom. "He says that every time he opens it." Tom said back to her. "I can't believe there is beer in this place." Amy replied. "I'm not sure it is beer." Evelyn giggled a little and said to Tom. "Remember the bacon Tom Carpenter. It's the same type of situation."

Amy asked. "What about the bacon dad?" Tom looked at Amy and in all seriousness he said to her. "I never run out." Amy laughed and said. "Well that's awesome dad." Tom replied to her. "I never buy any because I never run out."

Amy didn't laugh at his words this time. Instead, she got a serious look on her face as she looked to Evelyn who said to her. "He's okay Amy. He's just lost right now." John was still thinking on what Tom had said about not leaving Amy, so he jumped in and said to Tom. "Your daughter will be fine here with me while you find your wife." Tom just glanced at John and turned his attention to Amy who said to him. "He's right dad. John tells a lot of jokes, drinks beer and smokes like freight train. He tickles me when he talks about hunting bigfoot. But he's a really nice man."

Tom didn't want to hear anything about leaving Amy there, much less with a half drunk man. Tom said to Amy. "I can't just leave you here sweetie." Evelyn said to Tom. "You have to Tom Carpenter. You have to leave her here." Tom said to Evelyn with a forceful almost growling voice. "I can't leave her!" Evelyn walked over to stand in front of Tom and she said to him while giving him a very serious look. "You have no choice Tom Carpenter, if you want to find your Kristi."

Evelyn looked at Amy and said to her. "Your mother and father are soul mates. One will not live if the other doesn't survive. He will die Amy if he doesn't find her. He will die in both worlds." Tom stood up and said to both Amy and Evelyn. "Kristi wouldn't want me to leave our daughter." Tom looked at Evelyn and said. "I just found her!" Tom turned to Amy and said to her. "I wanted so much to see you again, and here you are in front of me. Tell them sweetie. Tell them we must stay together."

Amy stood up, gave her dad a hug, then leaned back and said to him. "I love you more than anything in this world dad.

You know that. Just like I know you feel the same way. You don't have to say it, you show it. So show it to me now dad, because I need you to do something for me. I need you to help me dad." Tom took Amy's hands in his hands and quickly said to her. "I would do anything for you baby girl you know that."

Tom moved his eyes about for a moment getting a glance at the other two standing close by. Amy moved her hands to each side of Tom's cheeks and she said to him as he looked at her. "Dad, find mom. I need you to find mom. I love her too." Tom lowered and shook his head at the same time. Amy still had her hands on his face and lifted his head back to her and she continued. "You found me dad. You can find me again once you're with mom. I want to see her too." Amy raised her hand, pointing it at John and said. "I'll be okay here with John. You go find mom and come back to see me."

Tom said to her. "I'm not sure I'm comfortable leaving you here with that guy." John blew out a puff of smoke and said. "Your mother..." Evelyn stopped John, saying. "John don't." John gave Evelyn a quick look and then looked back at Tom who asked. "My mother what?" John continued. "Your mother didn't mind leaving you with me when you were little. As I recall you rather enjoyed our time together."

Amy moved her hands and Tom turned to face John as he asked. "Just who are you?" Tom looked to Evelyn but she had her head down with her chin against her chest. John continued as his eyes began to swell with tears. "Nothing would make me happier than to stay here with my granddaughter while you find your wife."

Tom looked John over real good and the thoughts of him talking about bigfoot set Tom to thinking it could be his dad, though he still doubted it. John walked over and grabbed Tom's right upper arm with his left hand as he said to Tom with a proud voice. "While my son, my hammerhead finds his wife."

There was a brief pause as Tom and John looked each other in the eyes. After the pause, Tom asked. "Are you really who you are claiming to be?" John smiled and Evelyn said to Tom as she nodded her head up and down. "He is Tom Carpenter." Tom said to John. "I never expected to see you again. It's been so long since you passed."

John replied. "I know all this is difficult to understand. I didn't expect to see you here either son. Things here, across the plane are almost never what they seem. There are no rules here like there are for the living."

Tom stood quiet as John spoke and in complete disbelief his father was there before him. When John finished talking, Tom reached his hand out to shake John's hand. John smiled, took Tom's hand in a handshake and pulled Tom into him to give him a hug as well.

Tom leaned back, broke the handshake and asked as he pointed his hand towards his daughter. "Have you been with her this whole time?" John looked at Amy and then back to Tom as he replied. "I felt her cross into this place. It was easy for me to find her and I've been by her side ever since."

Tom gave a quick nod and said to John. "Thank you. Thank you for keeping an eye on Amy for me." John replied. "You can thank me by finding your wife, and be kind to your mother when you see her again." Evelyn raised her head and looked at John when she heard what he said. Evelyn smiled at John though she didn't say anything.

Tom said to John. "So it's true? You came to her after you passed?" John replied. "I did. I had to see her again. I had to see you again even though you were asleep when I came." Tom lowered his head for a moment and then raised his face up and said to his father. "I thought she went crazy."

John laughed a little and then grew a serious look on his face as he said to Tom. "Love makes a person crazy at times. You being the man you have become, to have come so far for those you love is testament to that very statement." Tom looked at Evelyn then to Amy and back to John and said. "I think I understand now why mom done the things she did." Evelyn broke the moment when she said to Tom. "We need to go Tom; we are running out of time."

Amy walked over and without saying anything she wrapped her arms around her dad with the side of her face against his chest. Of course, Tom wrapped his arms around his little girl. Tom rested the side of his face on top of Amy's head with his eyes closed and he said to her. "I love you Amy." Amy replied without moving to break the hug. "I know dad. I love you too." Then Amy leaned back breaking the hug and she said to Tom. "Dad... I love mom too. I want to see her but I can't unless you find her okay. Go find mom for me dad. Do it for you and me so we can be together again."

Tom pulled Amy back in giving her another hug and he said to her. "I'll do whatever it takes sweetie. I promise." Amy looked up at Tom and said. "Keep the wooden nickels dad. You keep them this time and you can pay me for a hug the next time we see each other."

Tom had been holding the wooden nickels in his hand the whole time. He held out his hand and opened it. Tom and Amy both looked at the two wooden nickels for a moment. Then Amy reached out and used her hands to close her dad's hands around the nickels. Amy kept her hands around Tom's as she said to him. "These are the missing piece your soul you were searching for." Tom shook his head and said to Amy. "You are the part of me that was missing. It was you my sweet baby girl."

Evelyn said again to Tom. "We have to go Tom Carpenter. We have to go now!" Tom noticed the urgency of her voice. He looked at her but she was looking down the old dirt road. Tom looked in that direction and saw many of what looked like people walking towards them in the distant faded light from the light pole. Tom quickly said to Amy. "I'll be back sweetie." Amy replied. "Go dad. Hurry and find mom."

Evelyn grew anxious and said again with a sharp voice. "Tom! We have to go!" Tom knew time was against them; especially with the spirits getting closer to them. But Tom took a short moment to acknowledge his father one more time with a nod as he said. "Thanks dad." John didn't say anything. He just smiled with the proud look of a father. Amy walked back over and sat down on the bench while watching Tom. John walked over and stood beside Amy with a beer still in his hand.

Evelyn said to Tom. "Close your eyes." Tom took a good look at Amy and John for a brief moment and then he slowly closed his eyes though he only wanted to keep them on his daughter. Evelyn said to him. "Focus on your house. Remember the smell of the coffee in the pot."

Tom focused on the smell of fresh coffee, and the mug stamped #1 dad his daughter got him on fathers' day the year she died. Once the image got stuck in Tom's head he actually began to smell the coffee in the room as if it were just made. Then the silence and his focused state was interrupted by the familiar old raspy voice he had grown to know saying. "I didn't mean keep them closed forever."

CHAPTER 8

Tom opened his eyes to find he was still sitting in his chair at the table with his feet still in the pan but the water was now steaming. Evelyn moved her hands away from his neck area and smiled that old toothless smile at Tom.

Tom's eyes grew wide with confusion as he looked around for a moment and noticed the water steaming at his feet. He started to take them out but Evelyn stopped him by saying. "Don't move Tom Carpenter, don't move. I have to make sure nothing else comes through." Tom looked at her with a confused look and said. "Comes through?" Evelyn quickly asked. "Where's the salt? Where do you keep it?"

Without even thinking about it Tom replied. "In the spice rack in the cabinet to the right of the sink." Evelyn quickly made her way to get the salt from the cabinet. As she did, Tom said to her as he rubbed his neck and thinking about how strong she was. "You're a lot stronger than you look Evelyn." Evelyn replied as she retrieved the salt. "I work with my hands Tom Carpenter. I work with them every day." Then she walked back over to Tom and started pouring salt in the water around his feet as she said to him. "The water is a lubricant in the crossing Tom Carpenter. It is also a doorway others may use to get here. This place seems to be exempt from them, so we must keep it that way." After Evelyn poured the salt in the pan of water, she said to Tom. "You can take your feet out now Tom Carpenter. We should be okay."

Tom still looked confused and asked. "What do we need to keep that way? Why the salt? And why is this place different?" Old lady Evelyn put the salt away and sat down at the table to get a sip of her coffee. Then she said to Tom. "Drink your coffee Tom Carpenter before it gets cold." Tom looked down at his coffee mug and upon seeing that it was still steaming, he asked. "How is it possible that this coffee is still hot after we were gone for so long?" Tom gave Evelyn a both serious and confused look as he said to her. "Explain this stuff to me. I don't understand any of it. Was it all just a dream?"

Tom waited for just a moment and then it hit him. The wooden nickels his daughter gave him should be in his pocket. He leaned back in his seat and reached into his pants pocket and pulled out the two wooden nickels. Tom held them out in front of himself for Evelyn to see them. Then he said to her. "I have no idea how this is possible. But if I can bring these back with me, I can bring Amy back too." Tom looked desperately at Evelyn and asked. "Can't I?"

Evelyn said to Tom. "You cannot bring Amy back Tom Carpenter." Tom looked down at the wooden nickels as if they were evidence and then back to Evelyn who said. "It's not the same thing Tom Carpenter. Not the same at all. Amy won't leave where she is because she feels she belongs there. She would never come here Tom. Souls like Amy's have to be tricked. They have to be convinced there's a way for them to be alive again. Often times they have to believe they can live in someone else's body. That's why the others are always looking for you Tom. They want to come back. So For now, Amy will remain in purgatory."

Tom lowered his head in disappointment as he stared at the two wooden nickels he held in his hand. Evelyn continued. "The salt closes all doors Tom Carpenter. It was established as a protector during the destruction of Sodom and Gomorrah. As for your coffee still being hot, we never left Tom Carpenter and time doesn't count across the plane. Time doesn't exist there."

Tom said to her. "Only one question remains." Evelyn took a sip of her coffee and said. "There are many questions to answer; though we haven't got that far yet. As for this place being a safe place. Which is what you want answered. This place you recognize as your home is not your home. It is a place your mind has created to protect your soul for a short while. If you die Tom Carpenter, this place won't last and nor will you in the form you are in now."

Tom shook his head in disbelief and he said to the old lady. "Okay, I think we've gotten past what I am able to believe. This has all happened so fast I know. I can't explain how the wooden nickels came to be in my pocket but I can't bring Amy back. I know you tried to explain that to me Evelyn, but it's just hard for me to believe. And the hardest part for me to believe is that this whole place is only a vision of some kind my mind created. If that were true, then where am I in the physical form? Where am I Evelyn?"

Evelyn said to Tom. "I will show you soon enough Tom Carpenter. Please understand; I have to leave now. I have to go be with my granddaughter. I fear her condition isn't getting any better. Please, Tom Carpenter forgive me for not being able to help you anymore today." Tom asked. "Will you be back, or are you done?" Evelyn got up out of her chair and said to Tom. "Thank you for the coffee Tom Carpenter. We still have much to do before the end. I will return as soon as I can."

Tom was extremely disappointed the old woman had to leave, but being the nice guy he was, he asked if he could give Evelyn a ride home as they walked towards the door. Evelyn laughed a little and told Tom that she would be home as fast as the door lock clicked. Tom asked Evelyn how she would get home so fast. He still didn't understand that everything around him wasn't physically real. Evelyn said to him. "You don't listen very well do you Tom Carpenter?" Tom just smiled and Evelyn said to him. "Time doesn't count across the plane."

Tom said goodbye to Evelyn as she left the house and she just waved a hand at Tom as she carefully stepped down the cement steps of his front porch. Tom eased the door shut very slowly as he watched the old woman through the narrowing crack. When the door closed and he heard the click of the lock, Tom opened the door quickly and stuck his head outside. He truthfully expected to see the old lady still in the front yard but she was gone.

Tom was a little surprised that everything she told him was true, and the time not existing really had his attention. He whispered to himself as he nodded his head. "Time doesn't count." With that thought in mind Tom began to wonder just how long he may have actually been in his current situation. And how long had his wife Kristi really been trying to find him.

Tom shut the door and walked back to the kitchen to get his coffee mug. He filled it with fresh coffee from the pot and stood there at the counter looking toward the living area as his mind wondered. A lot had happened to him in a short time, and it was a lot to process. Tom took a few sips of his coffee and then walked to his daughter's room just as he had done many times before. Tom picked the skinny teddy bear up and hugged like a child would do and he said to it. "I found her skinny."

Tom sighed heavily and laid the teddy bear back on the bed. Afterwards he walked over to the picture of his daughter that was on the mirror and said to it. "I'll find a way Amy. Once I find your mother, I'll find a way to get you here." Tom rubbed the picture with his fingers and then turned to leave the room.

On his way out of the room Tom turned to look down the hall to the room at the end just passed the guest bathroom. He said to himself as he started towards the guest room. "Ah what the hell." Tom paused for a moment as he stood in front of the guest room door. Then he slowly reached out, grabbed the doorknob and tried to turn it but it was locked. Tom grabbed it with both hands and even shook it what he could, but he could not open the door. Once he let go of the doorknob and still standing there facing it, Tom said to himself. "Damn thing doesn't even have a lock; and been locked ever since I woke up here."

The doorknob of that room was supposed to be temporary. It was a cheap knob with no lock put on the door at the end of construction and was never changed. Tom couldn't figure how or why the door would appear locked and he wasn't able to get inside that room. And even though it frustrated him, he didn't try to open it again that day.

Tom wasn't sure what to do with himself the rest of the day since it was only around noon. Then a strange thought come over him. He remembered that he hadn't had breakfast that morning. Tom figured since he couldn't possibly run out of bacon, he might as well cook the whole package and snack on it through the day.

Tom done just that too. He cooked all of his bacon and had a plate rounded over when he sat down in his recliner to relax. This was very strange behavior for Tom Carpenter as he never ate inside the living area and was against it. But things were different for him now. And for the first time in a long while, he felt some confidence in what he was doing. He allowed hope to reenter his mind.

Tom didn't do anything else that day besides sit in his recliner and snack on the plate full of bacon. He wanted to watch the TV several times but wasn't going to get up and turn it on either. And unlike every other day, Tom didn't clean the dishes right away and wipe down the table. Instead, when it got late he went from his recliner to his bathroom to take a shower like he had done every evening before. That part was natural habit kicking in and Tom knew it but didn't resist it. He figured he done well to not get so wrapped up in routine that day.

When Tom got done with his shower he made his way to the kitchen in his plain pajamas and bathrobe. While there, he turned the coffee pot off and wiped down the table for the night. He couldn't resist letting it sit dirty through the night, but had no problem letting his dishes sit. Tom took a good look around the place for a moment and then went to lie down.

When he got into bed, he reached over and put the two wooden nickels on the pillow next to him where his wife would have slept. Tom looked up at the picture on the wall and said in a low voice. "I'm trying Kristi. Don't give up on me."

Tom laid there looking at the picture until his eyes burned too much to hold them open. The day had worn him down with everything and revelation that happened. So once his eyes shut, he almost instantly fell asleep.

During that night Tom didn't have the normal dreams he had before. On this particular night Tom had more of vision like experiences. At one point he saw himself running down an endless dark tunnel with only a faint light in the distance he couldn't seem to reach. During that vision and even though he was asleep; Tom felt the tunnel would cheat him for eternity and he would never reach the light at the end.

In a different vision, he saw old lady Evelyn Murray and Amy standing beside the bed of Evelyn's granddaughter Ashley. They were standing there watching the little girl sleep, and neither of them were saying anything. Tom felt as though Amy was going to welcome Ashley into Purgatory the way his father had done for her. Tom felt that once they enter into Purgatory, a way out may be impossible due to their feelings of belonging.

In the early morning hours of the night, Tom heard his wife's voice call out to him saying with low soft voice. "Open your eyes Tom... I'm right here if you will open your eyes." Tom rolled around in bed and sweated tremendously. At one point he saw the brightest flash of light he had seen thus far. The light was so bright it burned Tom's eyes and he couldn't look into it where his wife's voice was coming from. Tom tried each time he heard his wife call out, saying. "I'm right here Tom. Just open your eyes honey... I'm right here."

Tom tried and tried to call out her name but couldn't muster the strength to do so. At one point the vision got so powerful Tom was able to smell his wife's perfume. When that smell hit him, he gave it everything he had to call out her name.

Tom sat straight up in bed as he yelled his wife's name as if she was a mile away. Upon his own loud voice Tom opened his eyes only find an empty bedroom and himself covered in sweat. He sat there for a good while with his face in his hands feeling as if he had failed her. He felt so close to touching her, and the smell of her sting lingered around him.

Tom felt that he had also failed his daughter Amy by not being able to connect with his wife. After his moment of grief, Tom started repeating to himself in a whispering voice. "Don't give up. Don't give up. I got to keep going. Don't give up."

Tom got up that morning and without thinking about continued his day in the same routine he had done before Evelyn ever showed up. He kept the same routine for the next three days as he waited for Evelyn to return. Each night following those days was similar to one before. Eventually it became too much to sit and wait for someone who might or might not show up again. Tom began to feel there was no hope for Evelyn's return. He felt that he would have to go it alone if he wanted to find his wife.

On the morning of the fifth day, Tom broke the routine just after his usual breakfast. Once he was done eating, Tom put his dishes in the sink and said to himself. "To hell with waiting... She's old, something may have happened to her." Tom was convincing himself to cross the plane without Evelyn though he was nervous about doing it. However; Tom wasn't the type of man to let fear guide him. So he didn't waste a minute more before he got the turkey pan back out of the cabinets and as it filled with water, he put the salt on the table.

When the pan got around half full with lukewarm water, Tom put it on the floor and took a seat. He slid off his house slippers and slowly put his feet in the water while he closed his eyes. Tom focused hard on his wife but had no reference point of where she might be. He kept his eyes closed remembering what Evelyn had said about focusing on the black nothing behind his eyelids.

Tom had no idea of what to think about for a reference and was a little worried about thinking on anything. Evelyn had explained to him that letting one strange thought in his mind could lead him to somewhere he shouldn't be. The only thing that made any sense to Tom and had proven results was the light pole at the end of town. So Tom focused hard on the light pole and figured seeing his daughter again wouldn't a bad thing.

After a long while of sitting motionless and focusing as hard as he could, Tom opened his eyes. The scene he laid his eyes upon was not what he wanted to see. Tom hadn't gone anywhere. His feet were still in the water and he was sitting in his chair at the table. Great disappointment swept over him and Tom said to himself. "This is pointless." Frustrated, Tom stood up, grabbed the salt and headed towards the cabinet on the right side of the sink. Once he put the salt back where it belonged he turned around and gasps in surprise. His body was still sitting in the chair and the salt was still on the table.

Tom quickly remembered what Evelyn had told him about seeing himself in such a way. Tom's shock and surprise turned to excitement. He valued his deed as a great accomplishment though it may have been a mistake. Tom looked down and he was barefoot unlike before when his shoes were somehow on when he went with Evelyn across the plane. Tom made his way over to the table and he knelt down in front of his motionless body to pick up his shoes but he couldn't grab them. Tom's hand just kept going through the shoes because he wasn't a physical being and his shoes were. This confused Tom terribly because he was able to grab the wooden nickels from his daughter. Even after all Tom had been through he still couldn't distinguish the difference between the land of the living and astral plane.

Tom held his hands out to his sides as he gave himself a looking over and said out loud. "So here I go in my pajamas and barefoot. This should be interesting." At that moment a strange thought entered Tom's mind and his eyes wondered towards the hallway. Tom figured since he was in a ghost like form he could open that damn door at the end of the hall and see why he couldn't get into the guest bedroom. So Tom wasted no time in heading down the hall to the door of the guestroom. Tom whispered to himself. "Here goes nothing." He reached out slowly to take the doorknob in his hand but he quickly let go of it and growled.

The doorknob burned Tom's hand as if he gripped a hot coal from a campfire. This frustrated Tom badly. A burn is always a pain to deal with and slow to heal. For Tom it was a double shot of being pissed all at once. He didn't want to deal with a burn and he wanted that door open something terrible. But he didn't try anything else to enter that room even though he wanted to start kicking it down. Instead he went into the kitchen and began running cold water on his hand to help ease the pain. Tom let the water run on his hand for several moments before he got a cloth out of the drawer to wet and wrap his hand.

While holding his injured hand, Tom began to sweat and the air in the house felt thick and hard for him to breathe. So Tom walked to the front door of the house, opened it and stepped outside for some fresh air. It was dark out, but in the distance Tom could see the sky was starting to get slightly brighter in the east. Daylight would be coming soon. As Tom stood on the porch taking in the clean morning air, he looked to his left and the light pole and bench were within sight. This was very strange to Tom as the light pole was at the end of town over a mile from his house. Yet there it was less than a quarter mile away.

Tom looked to his right and saw the many different houses that lined the streets on both sides and looked completely like the town he knew. Tom took it as a sign, a guide of sorts that he should go investigate. So he shut the door to his house leaving it unlocked and he started down the street on his bare feet. Tom had no idea what he was doing, but was willing to try anything and everything it took to find his wife, or see his daughter Amy one more time.

CHAPTER 9

Tom walked down that old road where the broken pavement and potholes led to the dirt part of it and lonely light pole. Several times he stumbled as he would get a sharp piece of gravel under his bare feet, but he didn't stop and wouldn't have being the type of man he was. He continued down that road until he finally made it to the light pole where he took a seat on the bench. Tom rubbed his feet a little as he took a good look around.

There was nothing and nobody else there, and it was at this point Tom realized he had to worry about the other spirits that might be lingering about. With that in mind he only took a short rest until the pain in his feet subsided. Then Tom stood up, took a good look all around and figured he was most likely wasting his time there. So he turned back to the direction of his house to go home. Tom looked down the road in the direction he had come from and got a terrible shock. His porch light along with all the others weren't down that way anymore.

In the distance where his house should have been was only a faint light from what Tom could barely see was another lonely light pole. Tom turned around to look behind him down the old dirt part of the road and there was another lonely light pole about the same distance away. At this point the memory of what Evelyn said about the light poles going on forever stuck in Tom's mind. He said to himself. "Oh I've done it this time. You're a genius Tom Carpenter. Pure Genius not to wait for Evelyn."

In a slight panic Tom took off running toward the direction his house should have been but wasn't there anymore. He didn't make it far and the pavement ended in that direction too and he was now running on an old dirt road. Tom noticed it even though it was dark but didn't stop. Soon, he came to the other light pole and like the last one, nobody else was there. Tom looked around and again to only find another light pole in the distance. For Tom it was worth a shot to try. He figured he might get lucky and his daughter and dad would be at one of them. So he took off again toward the next light pole. Each time he took off for one of the light poles it seemed a lot further away than the last. Tom wasn't a young man anymore, and the loose rocks under his feet made the quarter mile journeys seem like multi-mile journeys.

This explains why when Tom got to that pole he was both out of breath and his feet were hurting badly from the sharp gravels in the road. Tom took a look at the pole, bench and all around again but no one was there. He looked back in the direction he came from at the other light pole and panic began to set in. Tom was looking around in every direction including into the forest and along the brushy fences that lined the road. In a frantic state of mind he said to himself. "I could be running in the wrong direction… But damn it, that way could be the wrong direction too."

Tom took another look around as his mind wondered about all the possibilities of things that could go wrong. His biggest fear was never being able to get back and not ever seeing his wife and daughter again. Tom looked to the next light pole down the road and said to himself. "I won't quit… I have to keep going… Just keep moving old man." Even though his feet were hurting, Tom took the pain and began to run to the next light pole.

When he got close to it he stopped running and just walked up to the light pole and bench. Evelyn's words of how it could go on forever rang loudly in his mind once again. Tom looked around just like he had been and then yelled out his daughter's name with a loud voice. "Amy! Amy where are you!" Tom called out over and over but there was no answer. There was only the silence of the predawn morning.

After several times of calling out for his daughter, Tom seemed to give up. He sat down on the bench leaned over with his face in his hands. He sat like that for a good spell and then started repeating to himself. "Don't give up Tom... Don't give up." As Tom sat on the bench trying to get his composure, he heard a faint voice in the morning breeze call out his name. But the faint voice was saying his name as Tommy and not Tom or Tom Carpenter that he was so use to.

Tom quickly sat up and began looking around but couldn't see anyone. From the sound of the voice whoever it might have been was a long ways away.

Tom heard the voice again coming through air very low, drawn out and faint, saying. "Tommy... Come back Tommy. You've gone too far."

Tom didn't like being called Tommy at all. It was what his mother called him when he was little and at times when he was grown. No one else called him by that name to his face so Tom figured the voice in the wind was his mother, but he couldn't be sure. Again, Tom looked around some more but had no idea how to get back. And he had no idea who was actually calling out to him.

Tom thought on how Evelyn had got him back before. So he sat down on the bench and closed his eyes. He focused hard on the warm water that should be at his feet and the smell of coffee that surrounded his kitchen. Tom reached a point where his mind was cleared and he wasn't imagining anything when he heard the old raspy voice of Evelyn Murray say. "Come back Tom Carpenter."

At the sound of her voice and with his eyes still closed; He saw a very bright flash of light that hurt his eyes. He leaned back feeling the back of what seemed to be his chair, but could have still been the bench. Tom shook his head and rubbed his eyes for a moment before opening them to a surprising sight.

Evelyn Murray had her face real close to Tom's and she was waving a small flashlight in his eyes. Tom said to her. "Okay, okay..." Evelyn backed up a little and began pouring the salt in the water around Tom's feet. Then she walked over to where she normally sat at the table and took a deep breath and let it out slowly while she looked angrily at Tom. Once Tom's eyes cleared he looked over at Evelyn and asked. "Are you okay Evelyn?"

The old woman just shook her head at Tom but didn't say anything. Tom knew she wasn't happy with what he done but he didn't want to sit in silence either. So he got up to take the pan to pour the water down the sink. But when Tom reached down to grab the pan his left hand quickly started hurting. Tom stood up straight and looked to find a circular burn on his palm. It was very strange to him that he would actually be burned. He couldn't figure how something that happened to his spiritual being would also happen to his physical being. Then he remembered something Evelyn said to him about that whole place just being something his mind created. At this point, Tom was getting himself confused.

He didn't say anything to Evelyn at that time about it. Instead he carefully took up the pan and went to pour it down the sink like he originally wanted to do. Afterwards Tom said to Evelyn. "I have to get some clothes on... I'll be out in a minute." Tom didn't feel comfortable walking around in his pajamas with anyone besides his family in the house. He was very modest and self-respecting that way.

Evelyn just sat quietly and didn't even look at Tom when he spoke. Tom gave her a quick look and then went into his room to get dressed. While Tom was getting his pants on, he heard Evelyn get up from the table. He wasn't sure what she was doing but figured she may be leaving because he made her mad. About the time Tom buttoned his pants he heard Evelyn's voice coming through his door saying with an angry tone. "You fool of a man Tom Carpenter! You know what you've done!?"

Tom was surprised she would try to talk to him while he was getting dressed so he replied. "Jesus lady, I'm getting dressed in here." Evelyn replied. "I'm not as forgiving as Jesus is Tom Carpenter! You fool! I don't know what to think of you anymore. I come save you from being so lost and I don't even get a thank you." Tom said loudly from behind the door. "Thank you Evelyn." Evelyn replied. "Huh... I'd leave your ass over there for a month or two if we weren't running out of time. Bet I wouldn't have to ask then! Would I?" Tom smiled real big and was glad Evelyn couldn't see it as he said to her. "No mam you wouldn't."

Tom walked over to his closet, got a black plane t-shirt and put it on while saying at the same time to Evelyn. "I know I shouldn't have gone without you, but I couldn't just sit around here and wait anymore. And I am really thankful you came to get me. Believe it or not I thought at one point it was my mother dearest but I should have known better." Tom grabbed a pair of socks from his dresser and then walked over to open the door as he asked. "What have I done Evelyn, tell me?"

Tom walked past Evelyn and went into the kitchen to sit in his chair and put his socks and boots on. Evelyn walked in there behind him, leaned against her usual chair and said. "This is no longer a safe place Tom Carpenter. No sir! Not anymore!" Tom asked. "What do you mean this isn't a safe place?" Evelyn quickly answered, saying. "You crossed the barrier which was your front door. You entered the outer realm and broke the barrier that protected this place.

To make it so a fool can understand it; you connected this place to the outer realm of the astral plane. Now spirits may find you here Tom Carpenter... Now we are really running out of time." Tom asked. "Then why use the salt this time?" Evelyn replied. "It still applies to those in other parts across the plane. Don't you ever listen to anything?"

Tom lowered his head and paused in thought for a moment before he continued to put his socks on. Then he said to Evelyn. "I know I should have waited for you. I got selfish and couldn't wait anymore. I know you had things you needed to do as well but..." Tom stopped and looked right at Evelyn and asked. "You being here now I have to ask and I hope it's okay... How is your granddaughter, Ashley?"

Evelyn pulled out the chair she was leaned against and took a seat before she said to Tom. "She's barely clinging to life Tom Carpenter... I feel blessed to get to see her even for a short time, but there really is nothing I can do for her. It's in God's hands now." Evelyn saw the burn on Tom's hand and how careful he was while using it so she asked. "Where were you trying to go that you shouldn't have been Tom Carpenter? Where did you try to go that caused that burn?"

Tom took a look toward the hallway and then back to Evelyn and said to her. "Ever since I woke up here, I haven't been able to open the guest bedroom door. I've tried almost every day but it's locked somehow without a lock on it. So I figured when I stood up out of my body..." Evelyn interrupted him by saying. "You figured you could walk right in." Tom nodded his head and said. "Yes, I did."

At the thought of it, Tom grew a confused look on his face and he asked Evelyn. "Why would a door like that be locked? Why can't I get in there? Do you know?" Evelyn sighed and seemed to regret answering. "Yes I do Tom Carpenter. I do know." Tom's eyes grew wide and he sat motionless for a moment staring at the old lady and then he said. "By all means, tell me why." Evelyn replied. "I'm not sure now is the right time."

Tom sat up straight, looked around for a minute and said. "You know Evelyn; I think you like to mess with me sometimes. You know if you build it up like that my curiosity is going to take over." Evelyn looked very seriously at Tom and said. "If I were messing with you Tom Carpenter, I would turn you into a frog." After she said it, she smiled and winked at Tom who just grinned and said. "I thought you said you weren't a witch like people claim." Evelyn smiled real big and said to Tom. "Well you're not sure I'm not a witch. So you better watch out." Tom and Evelyn laughed a little and Tom shook his head at how ornery the old lady was.

But the smiles didn't last long. Evelyn's smile turned to a frown and she said with a low deeply concerned voice. "Tom…" Tom knew what she was about to say would be serious and he replied with a serious voice. "Yes, Evelyn." The old woman lowered her head for just a moment and then looked up at Tom and said. "What lies behind that door is the truth your mind is protecting your soul from."

CHAPTER 10

Tom said to Evelyn in complete sincerity. "I need to know... I'm ready to know what that truth is." Evelyn looked at Tom real good with squinted eyes and said. "Maybe you are Tom Carpenter... Maybe you are." Tom looked toward the hallway and then back to Evelyn again and said as he was nodding his head. "If we can get that door open, I can handle whatever is on the other side." Evelyn asked Tom. "Do you want to know why the doorknob burned your hand Tom Carpenter? Do you want to know why I know it's the truth behind that door?" Tom gave Evelyn his complete attention and he said. "Yes, of course I want to know."

Evelyn leaned over the table a little toward Tom and said. "Only the truth can burn the soul my friend; only the truth." The two of them paused and kept their eyes fixed on the other for a while till Tom asked Evelyn. "So how do we open it?" Evelyn leaned back in her chair and said to Tom. "I can open the door for you Tom Carpenter that I can do." Tom quickly responded by saying as he stood up. "Well let's get to it. I'm ready." Evelyn eased up slowly saying at the same time. "I hope you are; I truly do."

Once Evelyn got stood up Tom started over towards the opening of the kitchen that led to the living area. He kept a watchful eye on Evelyn and could tell she was somewhat nervous about opening the door. Tom asked. "What is it Evelyn? What is that has you so worried?" Evelyn stopped, sighed heavily again and said. "Well, I guess I better tell you." Tom held his hands out a little from his sides and asked. "Tell me what?"

Evelyn leaned against her walking stick and lowered her head for a moment as she tried to think of an easy way to tell Tom what was behind the door. When she raised her head to look at Tom who could barely contain himself, she said. "I'm just going to say it, but don't you run back there and make a fool out of yourself Tom Carpenter. You listen and you listen good to everything I say before we walk in there." Tom couldn't wait anymore so he said asked in a very anxious way. "Will you tell me already!?"

Evelyn looked at Tom, clinched her jaws together and then said to him. "Your Kristi is behind that door."

Tom instantly gasped and turned to look down the hallway when Evelyn said in her old but forceful way. "Now Tom! Tom look at me!" Tom looked at her but only for a second and his attention turned back to the hallway. Evelyn walked over and grabbed Tom by the arm to get his attention. Tom was extremely anxious and breathing faster than normal when Evelyn said to him. "You won't be able to touch her Tom. She won't be able to hear you either. That door is doorway to another place. It's a place where we won't be seen or heard Tom Carpenter. This isn't like before with Amy. No it isn't. You hear me?"

Tom nodded his head but didn't say anything. Evelyn continued by saying. "Let's get on with it before you run back there and burn yourself alive trying to break that door down." Evelyn moved slow and at this point for the first time, it was driving Tom crazy. He would take a couple steps, stop and turn around to see how far Evelyn had come. For Tom it must have felt like forever to reach the guestroom door though it wasn't long at all.

As Tom got to Amy's room, he took a second to stop and take a look around since the door was already open. But Tom was so excited about his wife being so close he didn't stay at Amy's door very long. Evelyn stopped as well for a brief moment at Amy's room; and when she saw the skinny teddy bear lying on the bed, she whispered to herself. "Skinny." Evelyn quickly turned her attention to Tom and the door to guest bedroom as she hurried what she could down the hall. When Evelyn got to the door, she gave Tom a quick look and grin before she turned the knob to open the door for Tom.

The door to the room opened from right to left since the hallway was against the outer wall of the house and the rooms to the left. So when Evelyn opened the guestroom door, the first thing Tom saw was that it wasn't his guestroom at all. Instead he instantly recognized it as a hospital room. With the door only open a quarter of the way he saw the all too familiar counter, sink, glass door cabinets and contaminated waste disposal. As the door opened even more, Tom saw someone's feet sticking up from under the blankets on the hospital bed.

Evelyn was opening the door at a normal pace, but it felt like it was taking an eternity to Tom. He wanted to shove the door hard and fast so he could see if Kristi was in fact in the room; and if so then who was on the bed. At that moment in a time that didn't count; Tom Carpenter burned on the inside with desire to see his wife's face one more time.

Evelyn kept opening the door and Tom quickly saw a vital signs monitor next to the bed and the body of a man covered with the blankets. Further the door opened in what felt like slow motion to Tom; revealing the identity of the man lying on the bed. Tom's eyes opened wide with disbelief and utter shock when he saw his own body lying there with a bandage wrapped around his head. And in only a partial of second that seemed to be an hour for Tom; the door opened wide enough for him to see Kristi.

She was sitting in a sofa against the back wall of the room and close to the headboard of the bed. Kristi was wearing one of Tom's work shirts over a plane white undershirt and stained, partially torn blue jeans she normally only worked in around the house. She looked so tired and physically worn out. To Tom, she looked beautiful. Kristi was leaned over to the side with her head lying on the edge of the bed not far from Tom's and her right hand was resting on the chest of Tom's body.

Tom said out loud in the room but mainly just to himself as his eyes were teary and fixed on his wife. "My Kristi…" Tom started towards her as he was so excited to see her, but the lifeless appearance of his body grabbed his attention. He looked at Evelyn for an answer, but only for a moment as he couldn't take his eyes off of Kristi. Evelyn took a step closer to him and said. "You never actually came home after the wreck Tom Carpenter." Evelyn looked at his body and continued. "No you didn't… You're in a coma Tommy and you have been for a while."

Tom never looked away from Kristi and didn't catch that Evelyn called him Tommy; a name that he normally despised. Tom said to Evelyn without ever looking at her. "So this is the answer to all the riddles." Evelyn softly replied. "Almost Tom Carpenter, almost." Tom walked over real close to Kristi and Evelyn stopped him by saying. "If you touch her, it will only scare her. Don't drive her further away." Tom turned to Evelyn with his teary eyes and said with upmost sincerity. "What kind of hell is this place?"

Evelyn's eyes grew wide and Tom turned back to knelt down on his knees in front of his wife. Evelyn didn't reply but stood silent hoping he could resist touching Kristi. Tom whispered to Kristi even though he knew she couldn't hear him. "You're so beautiful." Tom paused as he just looked at his wife sitting there by his body waiting for him to wake up. After several moments passed, Tom said to Kristi. "I love you Kristie... I always will." Tom never took his eyes off of Kristi though it broke his heart more with every second he looked at her.

Eventually Tom stood up, turned to Evelyn and spoke over the huge lump in his throat as he pointed his hand toward Kristi. "It takes a hell of a woman to stay by her husband through something like this." Tom asked Evelyn. "How do I get back in my body? Or is this just some kind of hell to torture me further?"

Evelyn said to him. "It takes a strong man to not give up on his family when times get hard... It takes a hell of a man to be willing to cross the astral plane; and be willing to face the hurtful pains of the past

just to see his wife one more time.
Especially when he knows he won't be able
to touch her, speak with her or kiss and
hold her... Hell of a man indeed, Tom
Carpenter."

Tom looked at Evelyn in a disgusted
way and said to her sarcastically. "Hell of
man! Huh!" Tom pointed towards his wife
again and said. "I am nothing compared to
her. You know when she'll leave Evelyn? Do
you?" Evelyn said with a calm and almost
pleading voice. "I do Tom." Tom replied.
"Yea... I do too. After she falls over dead
she'll leave! Look at her Evelyn! She's tired,
pale and weak... She's so strong Evelyn!"

Tom paused as he took a good look
at his wife and then he continued, saying.
"She's stronger than anyone I know... She's
so beautiful." Tom nodded his head a
couple times while facing his wife and he
said with a low voice. "Hell of a woman."

Tom paused for a moment as he
admired his wife's strength and loyalty.
Then he turned, looked at his body lying
there on the bed. Tom turned to Evelyn for
a second and said in frustration with his
right hand pointed toward his body. "This
poor bastard isn't even strong enough to

open his eyes! Hell of a man lying there!"
Evelyn pleaded, saying. "Please Tom..."

Tom grew angry to the point he
became almost frightening for Evelyn. Tom
was a broad shouldered man with big hands
and his very demeanor while calm
demanded respect. It was easy to see why
most anyone would be intimidated by him
when he was angry. Tom began yelling to
his body at the same time he forcefully
slapped at the covered leg area. "Get up
hell of a man! Get up!" Tom repeatedly
tried to slap the legs of his body but he
couldn't physically touch them. His hands
would glide through each time as if the legs
weren't there at all.

Evelyn was almost too afraid to say
anything and certainly didn't want to touch
him. Tom was all heart, but that big heart
was broken. Tom leaned over just a little
with his arms bowed out as if he were
about to fight and he roared at his body
lying on the bed. "Get up damn you!" His
voice was loud and of course it scared
Evelyn enough she let out a yelp and drew
her arms in as if to protect herself.

Just after Tom's outburst, the vital
signs monitor began showing fast unusual
patterns in the body's heart rate. Tom

almost fainted and but resisted and stayed upright but wobbly. Evelyn rushed over and grabbed him. At the same time, Kristi bounced up out of her sofa and leaned over Tom's body saying. "It's okay Tom. It's okay. I'm right here sweetie." Watching her; Tom hurt even deeper inside and grew weaker.

The vital signs monitor started showing even more disturbing heart patterns. Kristi continued with as calm of a voice as she could muster though she was now weeping over Tom's body. "It's okay my wonderful man. Go rest if you must... It's okay Tom." It was clear in Kristi's words and voice that she was certain she was about to lose Tom forever. Evelyn yelled at Tom who was watching his wife be so strong as he grew weaker and more broken hearted by the moment. "You are killing each other! We have to go Tommy!"

Tom could barely stand on his own but he managed to gather enough strength to turn to his wife and say. "I love you Kristi." At almost the same time, only one word apart from each other Kristi said to Tom's body lying on the bed. "I love you Tom." Evelyn fought off her own tears and pulled at Tom to leave the room.

Just as the two of them got to the opening of the guestroom door there began to be many knocks and bangs at the front door of the house. Tom looked at Evelyn with questioning look though he already knew the answer. However; Evelyn gave it to him anyway when she said him. "We've run out of time... They have found us." Tom knew Evelyn was referring to other drifting spirits who wanted be alive again. Tom knew it but had hardened his heart to be okay with it. With each second that passed, Tom grew even weaker and a cold sweat covered his head and chest.

He asked Evelyn. "Can they hurt her?" Evelyn shut the door to the guestroom and said to Tom. "Like you, they won't be able to open the door. The other side of it where Kristi is, that's the land of the living. What many call reality Tom Carpenter. The reality is; many over there are more lost than you are." Tom smiled just a little and Evelyn gave him one in return with a quick wink. But the moment didn't last. More and more spirits who looked just like normal people began banging on the door, walls and breaking windows.

Tom asked as he was fighting to keep his eyes open and his skin was growing pale. "Will they hurt you?" Evelyn said to Tom. "They don't want me. I am here in a different form than you." Evelyn paused for a moment and Tom was leaning against the wall of the hallway with his hands on the wall helping him stay upright. Evelyn said to Tom. "You're going to die Tommy and there's nothing I can do about it." Tom nodded as his breathing got faster and he said. "I know... I know. But Kristi can move on if I'm gone. She can still have a life."

Tom glanced over at Evelyn hoping she would agree. However; Evelyn didn't deliver the news Tom wanted to hear when she said. "I'm afraid; it doesn't work that way Tom. She will die too." Tom was hurting bad and squatted down with his butt resting on his heels and his hands on the floor. Tom said to Evelyn with what little laugh he could gather through the pain and weakness. "Don't call me Tommy." Evelyn just smiled and Tom continued with his voice growing weaker as well. "It's time. I have to do this so she won't suffer anymore."

Tom looked to the front door and Evelyn grew concerned and asked. "You'll die to end her suffering?" Tom stood up slow, shaking and gritting his teeth and moaning as if he were picking up a thousand pounds with barbed wire ropes. He stood straight up with his shoulders out wide though his knees and body was slightly shaking and he said to Evelyn. "Every day." Tom turned and began wobbling down the hall just past Amy's room and he stood half slumped over leaning against the front door. Evelyn grew a lump in her throat and tears in her eyes as she said with a low sad voice. "Goodbye my friend, Tom Carpenter." Tom turned his head and started to say thank you but when he got turned to Evelyn's direction, she was gone.

At this point many of the spirits were trying to climb through the broken windows and the bangs and knocks against the front door and walls of the house grew louder than ever. Tom kept his left hand against the door to hold himself up as he reached his right hand in his pants pocket and pulled out the two wooden nickels. Tom held them to his lips, kissed them and said. "I'm sorry Amy."

Tom gripped the wooden nickels tight in his hand making a fist that he put against the door as he unlocked it with his other hand. He was fighting hard just to stay on his feet and desired to fall over and go to sleep more than he had ever felt before. Just to make sure he wouldn't lose them, Tom put the wooden nickels back in his pants pocket. Then he took hold of the doorknob of the front door, paused for a second and said. "For you Kristi."

CHAPTER 11

As Tom prepared to open the door, the noise being made by those outside was beginning to be deafening. Tom felt that he had no choice but to face them and end the suffering for both himself and his wife Kristi.

Tom turned the knob and quickly jerked the door open wide and let out a light growl at the same time; as he expected to be tackled. However; when the door opened everything fell silent. Tom stood in shock as the people standing before him were now motionless, and standing with their heads down.

As Tom stood still a sharp pain hit him and his body jerked as if he were being electrocuted. Tom leaned over and almost fell to the floor but was able to catch himself by grabbing the door jam. Tom looked up with his lungs barely drawing breath to see the spirits in the form of random people, all turn and look in the direction beyond Tom's yard to the east.

Tom pulled himself back up and took a step out toward his front porch. When he did, the people standing there parted and made an aisle towards the yard. Tom took another step and was completely out of his house when another more powerful shock and pain hit him. This time, Tom let out a loud growl and stumbled forward, falling to his knees at the edge of the porch by the steps.

Tom was in serious pain, and sweating badly. To him the dew covered grass in the yard looked very inviting to lie down on. Tom started crawling one hand and knee moving forward after another. It was a slow crawl as Tom barely had enough strength to hold back his body as he made his way down the steps.

Just as Tom's right hand touched the grass there was a loud, earth shaking rolling thunder overhead. The people standing there around Tom began to back up further and further until they faded away into the darkness. In just a few short moments after the sound of thunder, Tom was alone lying on his back in the dew covered grass of his front yard.

Just as the pain of the electrifying shock began to subside; another sharp but different pain hit Tom in the chest and heart. Tom screamed in pain as his hands instantly reached up and cupped around his heart area. Again, a loud thunder rolled overhead.

Tom rolled over onto his right side facing the east. Tom expected to see the houses that normally lined that side of the street, but they weren't there. Passed Tom's front yard was nothing but an empty void except in the far distance. Tom could see a faint red sky and storm clouds over a mountain range that was never there before. To Tom it was a beautiful sight. It was as if it were a painting of an evening sun that had set behind the range of mountains. In a strange way, it relaxed Tom's anxiousness. But as each heartbeat passed, Tom grew weaker and even more pale than ever. His eyes began to lose color as he said in a very low, weak almost whispering voice. "Please."

Tom's body began to slowly relax and his muscles loosened all over. At that moment Tom was no longer able to see the mountain range or the red sky over them. He couldn't see anything and had grown numb all over. Darkness fell over him. And in that darkness, Tom remembered something Evelyn had said to him. She once told him that if he could focus hard enough on the nothing, then he could be anywhere with a simple thought.

As Tom was moments away from dying both in life and in spirit, a memory popped into his head as if he were living it. Tom remembered a time when his daughter was alive and around the age of fourteen. In the memory; Tom walked in the house and saw his wife Kristi sitting with Amy at the kitchen table having a serious conversation about something.

Tom didn't know what it was about and didn't really want to know if it had to do with women problems. Instead, he just stood at the front door watching his wife be a wonderful mother to their daughter. And in only a few moments after Tom had entered the room, Amy gave Kristi a hug and said. "Thanks mom." After the hug both of Tom's favorite girls looked to him and smiled. It was the smile on both their faces that Tom was holding onto.

A tear rolled out of Tom's left eye and rested for a second on the bridge of his nose. It was the last effort given by Tom Carpenter's big heart. And after just a few seconds passed, the tear fell and hit the ground. When it did, a very bright and powerful light shined down on Tom

Carpenter. He was no longer in what appeared to be his yard. Now he was lying down in a never ending white light. The blinding light was everything and everywhere. Nothing else could be seen besides Tom lying down on his side.

Tom began to breathe a little and feeling came back into his body as his legs slowly stretched out. And even with his eyes shut the light was so bright it was hurting them. Tom covered his eyes with his hands and rolled over on his back.

He wasn't sure, but thought it had to be the crossing over that Evelyn had talked about. Tom grew nervous, and at the same time quite surprised that he wasn't in any more pain except for the light that was ever so blinding.

Then the memory of how it all ended came back to him. Tom remembered that he wasn't able to get to his wife and so his daughter could see her again. With that thought the instant feeling of failure swept over him. He took a few deep breaths and then yelled out long and loud as if he were yelling beyond a crowd of noisy people. "Kristi!"

Tom kept his eyes covered and slowly regained his strength. Then Tom said to himself. "I don't want to be here without you." To Tom's complete surprise he heard his wife say with a low calming voice. "You won't have to Tom. I'm right here."

Tom tried to open his eyes to see her but there was only the light. He couldn't see anything and it hurt to even move his hands while his eyes were shut. Tom said out loud but in a low voice as he tried to reassure himself of what he heard. "Kristi… Are you there?"

There was no response this time and the light began to fade. Tom cracked his fingers apart just a little but kept his eyes shut. When he did, his eyes didn't hurt from the light. So Tom moved his hands from his face and his eyes still didn't hurt. Then he just slightly opened his eyes and he saw a bright light but not near as bright as before.

Tom repeated opening and shutting his eyes until he was able to keep them open for seconds at a time. He wanted so badly to be able to see. He had to know if Kristi was in fact there beside him. At this point, he figured he had to have reentered his body. Eventually the ever so bright light above him dimmed into nothing more than a light bulb on the ceiling of a room.

Tom focused in on the bulb and the plane drywall ceiling for a moment in disbelief that little light had been so bright before, and that he was lying on a bed and not in the front yard. He looked down the wall toward the foot of the bed and instantly recognized the dark blue curtains on the sides of the grey trimmed window. He was in the guest bedroom.

Tom looked to his left and there was the large cherry dresser with twelve drawers he built several years before. Tom sat up and looked to his right and for the first time, he saw himself in the mirror on top of the smaller dresser he had built. Also on top of the little dresser was a change of clothes that were obviously his. Tom noticed in the reflection that his head was wrapped with a bandage just like what he saw when he was with Evelyn. This excited him. He started to let himself believe he had reentered his body.

Tom threw the blankets back and quickly got out of bed and made his way over to the dresser to get his clothes on. Once he was dressed, he had to see what happened to his head. So he leaned over a little and slowly started to unwrap the bandage as he watched in the mirror. He was being very careful in case there was an injury even though he couldn't feel anything or see any blood spots on the bandage. Eventually he got tired of unwrapping it and he slowly but carefully pulled the whole bandage off of his head.

Tom sat the pile of bandaging down on the dresser and carefully began rubbing his head as he checked for cuts and other injuries that may be there. He checked real good but didn't find anything. So he put a little pressure down and rubbed his fingers through his hair and all over his head. He never found a single thing to warrant the bandage.

Tom looked over to the door and quickly walked to it but paused for a second before he opened it. The thoughts of all of it being a dream came over him. Just to make sure, Tom reached into his pocket to check for the wooden nickels. If he was in fact back in his body there would be no way he could have them since he buried them with Amy.

He knew it was a long shot to find the nickels considering the clothes on the dresser were clean and folded. But Tom had gotten use to the wooden nickels being in his pocket so he had to check. There was nothing in his right pocket and just to make sure he wasn't misremembering, he checked his left pocket too. That pocket like the other one was empty.

Tom's confidence in his situation grew. He slowly but gently grabbed the doorknob to see if it would burn him but it didn't. Still being cautious, he eased the door open and looked down the hallway. There wasn't a sound that he could hear anywhere in the house.

Tom started down the hall in a slow and cautious way till he got to Amy's door which was open. Tom stopped and looked inside. Skinny was still under the blankets with his head sticking out and everything looked just as he remembered and left it. Tom wanted more than anything for his current state not be like it was before which was a false reality. He was nervous about going into the living area and kitchen to find that he would be alone again.

Furthermore; he was terrified at the idea there would be only three strips of bacon gone from the package and nine eggs remaining in the carton. For Tom that would be the ultimate test. But being the man he was he didn't cater to fear. Tom started to walk into the living area and began hearing water running in the sink.

His heart began to pound in his chest as he desperately wanted it to be Kristi in there. Tom cautiously made his way to the double door opening between the kitchen and living area. Very slowly he took one small step after another until he made it far enough to see into the kitchen. There was a woman standing at the sink looking out of the window above it.

Tom's heart pounded hard with excitement. He knew exactly who it was even though she wasn't facing him. Her sandy blonde hair and figure although covered with a light blue short sleeve shirt and faded blue jeans gave her away. It was Kristi running water in the coffee pot. Tom stood still and began to shake a little as shock came over him.

He couldn't believe after all he had been through that he actually made it back. Part of him wondered if it was real at all, or if she would be able to see and hear him. He didn't say anything or move as he couldn't at the time. Instead, he just stood still watching her with his heart pounding.

When the pot got full, Kristi turned the water off, picked up the pot and began to turn to her left toward the coffee maker that was sitting on the counter. Once her body turned to the side, she stopped suddenly with the pot still in her hand. The image of someone caught her attention from out of the corner of her eye. Her breathing got faster and she was almost too afraid to look. Like Tom she was afraid it might just be a dream.

Kristi faced her doubts and turned slowly to face Tom who was standing in the opening and lightly shaking. She slowly reached out and sat the pot on the counter without ever taking her eyes off of Tom. Once the pot was out of her hand she turned her body and was completely facing her husband for the first time in what seemed a lifetime to both of them.

Tom could tell that she could see him but a small part of him still wasn't quite sure. He still thought it might be a trick of some kind played on him by the astral plane. He needed just one thing more to be sure, and Kristi gave it to him. With her now tear filled eyes and shaky voice she said to him. "I love you Tom."

Upon hearing her words it became real for Tom Carpenter and too much at the same time. He wilted to the floor and sat on his butt with his legs curled to the side. He had a blank hollow look in his eyes as the shock of it all overcame him. Kristi ran over and kneeled down beside him and threw her arms around his neck and shoulders. She put her right hand on the back of Tom's head and pulled him into her chest as her head rested on top of his.

Tom's hands rested on the floor as he was powerless due to the shock of actually being with his wife and the journey across the plane being over. Kristi said to him. "It's over Tom... You don't have to hurt anymore. I'm right here." Her words seemed to bring Tom slightly out of the state of shock he was in. He moved his hands a little and he didn't have such a hollow look anymore. But it was when the smell of Kristi's hair hit Tom that he knew for sure the nightmare was over.

Tom sat up a little straighter, wrapped his arms around Kristi and said to her as he kept her cheek next to his. "I'm so sorry Kristi." Kristi was rubbing Tom's arms up and down and crying at the same time in joy rather than pain. Tom started to break down as he said while still holding onto her. "I tried everything."

Kristi leaned back and saw the hurt on Tom's face. She wanted to assure him that everything was okay but Tom spoke first saying over the huge lump in his throat and tear filled eyes. "I tried and nothing worked." Tom took several fast breaths of air and Kristi took his hands in hers. Tom continued, saying. "I gave up in the end... I failed you when you needed me most."

Tom's head lowered as he wept in disappointment at himself and the overwhelming emotion of being in his wife's arms. Kristi was holding strong for him, even though tears ran down her face. She put her hands on his cheeks and said. "Tom. Look at me." Tom didn't raise his head, for he felt ashamed that he didn't do better for her.

Kristi said to him as she lifted his head. "Look at me Tom." Tom did raise his head that time and his jaws were clinched tight as he tried to hold himself together. Kristi said to him. "You didn't fail me Tom... You found me." Kristi pulled Tom in close, kissed him and rested her forehead against his and said. "I was in a dark place Tom and couldn't see anything. I was so afraid for I was so alone. Then I heard your voice call out to me. It was you Tom who saved me."

Tom grew a little confused; so he leaned back, kissed Amy's forehead and asked. "Why were you in a dark place sweetie?" Kristi took Tom's hands and said. "You were having trouble, and I thought I was going to lose you. The very thought of it was too much to bear. I remember collapsing to the floor and passing out. It was your voice that brought me back. When I woke up, you were still in the bed. I knew our journey wasn't over. I could feel we had another chance and now we are together again."

Tom didn't quite understand it but didn't question it either. He said to Kristi. "I was so afraid I lost you, Kristi." Tom smothered Kristi with his arms wrapped around her as he kissed her again and said. "I'll never let you out of my arms again." Kristi kissed Tom, looked him in the eyes and said. "Then don't."

Tom pulled Kristi to the floor with him as he laid down on his back. Kristi was lying beside him with her head resting on his chest. Tom ran his hands up and down her back and indulged in the smell of her hair he had longed to smell and touch again. Kristi who had been taking care of him was just glad that he was awake and able to hold her again. To her there was no place she rather be than held prisoner by Tom's arms.

For Tom Carpenter who had spent so much time with a broken heart, it was finally time to heal. As they were lying there on the floor; both of them thought of all the things that had happened to them and how strange it all was. In those moments as they embraced each other the life they once knew of being alone now only seemed to be a bad dream. Though Tom didn't say anything, he was most happy that he might still have a chance to take Kristi to see their daughter one more time.

CHAPTER 12

The two of them spent that evening showing each other the love they couldn't describe with words. While they tried to sleep, both Tom and Kristi would wake up at random times during the night just to make sure the other one was still there. Any time Kristi or Tom woke to find they had scooted away from the other; they would instantly and gently slide back towards the other one. Neither slept very well as they were both afraid of waking to find the other one gone again.

When daylight came the next morning; Kristi woke up to find she was lying on Tom's upper arm and had salivated all over it. She looked up at Tom and found him staring at the portrait of her, Amy and Tom on the wall. She didn't say anything even though she wanted to move and clean up the mess she made on his arm. Eventually Tom looked over at her which was a relief for Kristi. She picked her head up and used a blanket to wipe Tom's arm with. Tom said to her. "Oh I'm not worried about that sweetie. You were sleeping so well. Though I have to admit I'm glad you're awake because I really have to pee."

Kristi giggled, wiped the corners of her mouth and said. "It's still gross Tom." Tom just laughed and shook his head a little. Kristi said to him. "It's so nice to hear you laugh." Tom replied. "Well good loving does put a person in a better mood." Kristi smiled and laid her head on Tom's chest and said. "Still can't believe you're here. I can't sleep without you next to me."

Tom said to her. "The only way I could fall asleep without you was to put one of your shirts around my pillow." Kristi smiled real big and then raised her head to look at Tom and say. "I know. Your mom told me. But don't worry, I do the same thing." Tom got a confused look on his face and asked. "How would my mother know that? The only one who ever knew was old lady Evelyn Murray."

Kristi replied. "Well your mother and Evelyn were good friends. I guess Evelyn told her." Tom said with a half way grin. "That Evelyn sure is a mess. What did you think of Evelyn when you first met her?"

Kristi got a weird look on her face and she said to Tom. "Uh, I never met her." Then Kristi sat up, patted Tom on the chest and said. "Come on, I'll make us some coffee."

Kristi got out of bed wearing the same t-shirt she had on the day before, and white pajama bottoms with red hearts on them. Once she was out of the bed she didn't waste a second heading for the kitchen to get the coffee going. Tom on the other hand was slow getting up. Not that he was hurt, but his mind was beginning to wonder. Especially about Evelyn saying if his wife wouldn't leave her alone then she wouldn't leave him alone. It just didn't make any sense.

When Tom did get out of bed, he didn't have any clothes on, but quickly grabbed his pants and put them on and went to use the restroom. When he was done in there he grabbed a white short sleeve shirt from the closet, put it on and headed for the dresser to get some socks. The whole time his mind was wondering about how it was possible for Kristi to have never met Evelyn Murray.

Once Tom was dressed he made his way into the kitchen and asked Kristi. "So you never met Evelyn?" Kristi smiled as she

was making the coffee and said. "No I asked
your mom for help and she went to see
Evelyn for some advice. I do know that
much." Tom nodded his head and replied.
"Oh, okay... Well I got to meet her."

Kristi asked. "Isn't she like a witch or
something like that?" Tom frowned and
said. "No. She's just old." Kristi saw the
frown, laughed a little and said. "I didn't
mean to upset you honey." Tom smiled at
Kristi and said. "Oh no sweetie, don't think
that. I actually asked her the same thing
when we first met. Understand though, she
became a very good friend to me and
helped me so much to get back here. In
fact, I really don't think I would've woke up
if it wasn't for Evelyn."

Kristi asked just as she finished with
the coffee maker and hit the on button. "Oh
yea; what did she help you with?" Tom
stood next to the table but didn't say
anything. He wasn't sure if it was the right
time to tell Kristi he had seen Amy and his
father or not. Kristi saw that he was
thinking on something important and she
calmly said his name to get his attention.
Tom looked at Kristi and said. "Promise you
won't get upset?" Kristi replied. "No Tom I
won't. Or I'll try not to. Let's just put that

way. Tom said with the upmost sincerity. "She took me to see Amy."

Kristi got a saddened look on her face and she pulled a chair back at the table and sat down. Tom watched and knew that his words hurt her a little bit. After a brief moment, Tom took a seat on the other side where Evelyn normally sat so he could face her. Kristi looked at Tom very seriously but confused and said. "I know you Tom... I know how mad stuff like that makes you when your mother used to say that sort of thing. I know you would never lie to me as well."

Tom stopped Kristi by saying. "You're right sweetie. I would never lie to you. And yes, it used to piss me off when mom would talk about seeing dad after he passed." Tom leaned forward and reached his hands out to take Kristi's. She put her hands in his and Tom said to her while looking her in the eyes. "I saw her Kristi, along with my dad."

Tom paused for a moment and then he continued. "Amy asked me to bring you to see her. She wants to see you again. To make sure I would come back, she gave me the two wooden nickels I buried with her. I kept them for a long time but they didn't seem to make it back with me."

Kristi looked down into her cup for a moment and then she looked up at Tom and said. "I believe you Tom. I believe because there is no other explanation for them." Now it was Tom who had a confused look upon his face as he curiously said. "Them?"

Kristi got up without saying anything and went to the refrigerator and got something small off of the top she kept cupped in her hands. Once she sat down she said to Tom before revealing what she had. "Just before I collapsed in the hospital as you were having serious trouble; I saw your hand clinched tight. I reached out to take your hand but I had to pry your hand open. When I did; these fell into my hand." Kristi reached her arm out on the table with her closed palm turned up and she opened her hand showing Tom the two wooden nickels.

Tom gasped and slowly reached out as Kristi dropped them in his hand. Tom took a good look at them and asked. "How is something like this possible?" Kristi replied. "I'm really not sure, except maybe one thing." Tom asked. "What?" Kristi replied. "Your mother once said to me. "When you cross the plane, you always bring something back. Sometimes without knowing what it may be." Tom said to her. "I rather it be Amy who came back."

Kristi didn't say anything as she hoped the subject of her daughter would quickly end. It was hurtful to both her and Tom and she didn't want old pains to ruin the happiness of them two being back together. With that in mind, Kristi said to Tom. "So this Evelyn woman, do I get to meet her?"

Tom knew it was a sly move to change the subject and he was okay with it. He smiled at Kristi and jokingly said. "I don't know. I normally don't introduce new women in my life to my wife. I've heard that's not a good idea." Kristi laughed and said. "Tom Carpenter, I had no idea you liked them old." Tom grinned a little and replied. "They can't run away as fast." Kristi laughed and shook her head as Kristi got up to start breakfast. She turned to Tom with a smile on her face and said. "You're a mess."

Tom got up, put the nickels in his pants pocket, walked up behind Kristi and put his arms around her as he said to her. "I'm your mess." Kristi leaned her head back and to the side against Tom's and she said to him. "And I love it." Tom did want Kristi to meet Evelyn so he said to her. "Maybe after breakfast we can go to Evelyn's house and see if she's home." Kristi replied while still basking in Tom's grasp. "How about we just stay inside today? I'm sure we can think of something to do." Tom whispered to her as he slid his right hand up from her stomach to just underneath her breast. "Maybe breakfast can wait." Kristi laughed and broke Tom's grasp, turned around and kissed him before she said to him. "No it can't. I'm hungry and you need to eat too mister."

Tom sighed and settled for a cup of coffee. After filling his cup he went back to the table to sit down. Kristi was laying out pans on the stove and getting ready to fry some eggs when she stopped and stood motionless for a moment. Her stillness caught Tom's attention. He didn't say anything but kept his eyes on her. Kristi eventually turned around and asked Tom. "How'd she look when you saw her?"

Tom sat his cup down on the table as he said to his wife. "She looked good honey. She looked bored, but good. She's okay Kristi." Kristi nodded her head and said. "I have to see her." Tom replied with a serious look on his face as he kept his eyes locked with Kristi's. "I know." Kristi said to him. "Let's go see Evelyn after we eat if we can." Tom said to her as he could see the pain in her eyes. "Let's do that."

CHAPTER 13

Not much else was said between Tom and Kristi during their breakfast. The thoughts of going across the plane to see their daughter kept both their minds racing too much for conversation. However; there is something about the smell of a good breakfast that seems to draw a crowd.

When Tom and Kristi had finished eating; Kristi got up to put their dishes in the sink as Tom said to her. "Believe I'll watch a little TV to let my food settle before we take off." Kristi smiled and replied. "Okay Tom. If you get bored in there you can help with the dishes." Tom grinned and said. "I'll be sure to keep that in mind."

Kristi just shook her head as she giggled a little at Tom. She turned to the sink while saying to herself, but loud enough for Tom to hear her. "A mess I tell you." Tom just smiled to himself and walked over to turn on the TV manually because he couldn't find the remote anywhere. Just as he leaned over and reached his arm out to turn it on there was a knock at the door.

Tom stood up and looked at Kristi who was looking back at him and also wondering who would be there that early in the morning. Tom started towards the door and there was another three tap knock. Tom called out. "I'm coming!" Kristi stepped into the opening that divided the kitchen from the living area and waited to see who it was.

Tom opened the door and a smile instantly grew on his face. Evelyn Murray had come to see them, and she wasn't alone. Evelyn was dressed as usual with a multicolored muumuu, house slippers and that old grey poncho. And like many times before; she was leaning on her staff she claimed was only a stick she found in the yard. This time Evelyn had a large handbag with her and Tom could see something wrapped in brown paper barely sticking out of it, but he didn't think too much about it. Tom could also see someone behind Evelyn but couldn't see who it was so he just said to her. "What brings you by this morning?" Evelyn replied. "Do you remember me Tom Carpenter?"

Tom got a strange look on his face as he responded. "Of course I remember you Evelyn." Evelyn smiled with that old toothless smile that only and elderly person can acquire and she said to Tom. "Well then you know the smell of those eggs and bacon is something I can't resist."

Kristi could hear them but couldn't see the old woman for the door being open to Tom's right. So she made her way in there and stood next to Tom who quickly introduced her saying. "Evelyn, this is my wife Kristi. She asked just this morning if she could meet you. So we're very glad you are here."

Evelyn looked at Kristi and said. "It is I who is happy and honored to be here to meet you." As they the two women were meeting for the first time it began to lightly sprinkle outside. Kristi smiled and lightly slapped Tom on the shoulder as she said to him. "Well invite her in, don't let her just stand there. It's about to rain and I bet Evelyn doesn't want to stand in the rain Tom." Evelyn replied to Kristi saying. "He's good at that. Letting a person stand at the door. He surely is."

Kristi walked into the middle of the living area to give Evelyn some space as she came in, and Tom stood by the door to close it after Evelyn and her company entered. Evelyn started to slowly make her way in and Tom was waiting to see who she had with her. Evelyn stepped up to the outer edge of the door real close to Tom and she said to both Tom and Kristi. "I have a very special guest who wanted to come see you two if that's okay."

Tom and Kristi both nodded and told Evelyn it was alright. Evelyn looked at Tom and gave him that ole ornery and familiar wink. Tom knew she was up to something but wasn't quite sure what it was. Evelyn stepped past Tom and entered the living area where Kristi gave her a hug as she waited to see who the guest might be.

Tom looked and saw a young teenage girl standing on the porch with dark hair, wearing a plane long sleeve shirt and jeans. The girl looked up at Tom with a grin on her face and Tom said to her; revealing to Kristi who the other guest was. "Well I'll be. How are you Ashley?" Tom couldn't believe it. According Evelyn the last time he asked about Ashley it wasn't looking good for her. Tom never figured he would ever see her again.

Ashley replied to Tom, saying. "I'm much better now. Thanks you for asking." Tom and Kristi always liked Ashley as she was a sweet girl who never seemed to cause any trouble. Tom held his hand out toward the living area and Ashley quickly stepped inside. Kristi held her arms out insisting on a hug and to show Ashley she was more than welcome to be there.

Ashley walked over and hugged and Kristi. Tom caught a glimpse of Evelyn's orneriness showing as she had that look of secrecy when she winked at Ashley, but he didn't say anything. Kristi kept her arms around Ashley as she said to her. "I heard you were very sick Ashley. I'm so glad to see you're feeling better." Ashley replied. "I do feel better now. Thank you."

Evelyn broke the moment by asking. "Do you have any coffee made Tom or have you been lazy this morning?" Tom laughed but it was Kristi who responded by saying. "Oh yes, he's been lazy this morning, but I do have some coffee." Kristi let go of Ashley and went into the kitchen to prepare a cup for Evelyn who followed her in there.

Before closing the front door, Tom took a good look to the sky. Several of the light sprinkles hit him in the face as he closed his eyes and took a deep breath. He hadn't been able to smell the fresh summer rain since his daughter passed away years ago. But Tom wanted it badly. With his deep breath through his nose, he smelled it but only for a split second and it was gone. He just groaned a little and figured it was just his imagination so he went ahead and closed the door.

Once the door was closed, Tom walked over and stood by Ashley as he asked her. "You want to feed my fish today? They haven't eaten this morning?" Ashley quickly wrapped her arms around Tom's waist and said to him. "Maybe in a little while. I just want to visit with you and Kristi for now if it's okay."

Tom didn't know what to think about the hug. For a moment he stood with his arms out to his sides. The only thing he could figure, she was just very happy not to be in a hospital anymore. But after a moment, Tom put his left arm around Ashley's shoulder and hugged her back. Kristi periodically saw all this and thought it was cute that Tom had such a friend in the little girl. Though she thought it was strange for Ashley to hug him as if she was reunited with a lost friend.

Tom and Ashley joined Evelyn and Kristi in the kitchen. Evelyn sat with her back to the living area in her usual spot with her bag in her lap. Kristi got them all coffee and sat down across the table from Evelyn. Tom sat down at the head of the table this time since the two women had taken the first seats down on both sides.

Kristi asked Ashley. "Do want something to drink Ashley?" Ashley responded. "I would take a glass of milk if you wouldn't mind putting a spoonful of sugar in it." Her words stopped Kristi dead in her tracks and Kristi looked to Tom who was looking back at her. Evelyn had her cup up to her lips as her eyes wondered back and forth from Tom and Ashley who was standing to his right.

It caught them off guard and stunned them as that was the way their daughter Amy always drank her milk. She wouldn't have it any other way. Kristi swallowed hard and said to Ashley. "Of course sweetie, it's not a problem."

Kristi made the glass of milk for Ashley and said as she handed it to her. "You can have a seat if you want to." Ashley replied, saying. "Oh I've been sitting and lying down for a long time. I rather stand if it doesn't bother you." Kristi smiled in almost disbelief at how well-mannered the girl was. Kristi said to her. "You can do whatever you like Ashley, just make yourself at home."

Evelyn quickly said to Tom and Kristi. "That's something I need to talk to you about." Her statement grew some confusion among Tom and Kristi and Evelyn saw that it did. So Evelyn turned to Ashley and said. "I need to talk to Tom and Kristi for a minute. I'm sure Tom wouldn't mind if you went outside to feed his fish." Tom already offered that and she wasn't too interested in it.

So Tom said to Ashley. "I can do better than that." Tom pointed toward the hallway, gave Kristi a quick look and founded her nodding her head in approval. He said to Ashley. "First door on the left down the hall is our daughter's room. I'm sure you can find some stuff in there that will interest you." Ashley replied. "Okay, thank you." Tom responded, saying. "You're welcome sweetie."

Ashley took off for the room with her glass of milk still in hand. Tom turned to

Kristi and said in a low voice so Ashley wouldn't hear him. "It's been long enough. Someone needs to make use of Amy's stuff." It was hard for Kristi, but she acknowledged that Tom was right when she said to him. "I know, but it still feels like she might come home someday."

Evelyn again held her cup up to her lips to conceal a slight grin and she whispered to herself. "How right you are." Tom heard her say something but didn't make it out. He asked. "I'm sorry, what was that?" Evelyn replied. "I just said to myself the coffee sure was good. That's all Tom Carpenter." Tom gave her a strange look and Evelyn smiled at him with pure orneriness.

Tom asked. "What did you want to talk to us about this morning Evelyn?" Evelyn's smile went away and she said to both Tom and Kristi. "I know you both very well even though you barely know me." She looked at Tom and continued. "I've seen the love in your heart, along with the pain of loss." Evelyn looked back and forth at Tom and Kristi as she continued, saying. "Ashley is doing fine, just fine. But I am old. I may be too old to raise another child."

Evelyn saw Kristi was having a hard time with what she was suggesting so she said. "Now, I'm not trying to replace your daughter. I just thought you two might have gotten tired of an empty house. Maybe you would enjoy the role of parenting once again."

Tom didn't want to put so much pressure on Kristi by wanting a decision at that moment, so he tweaked the subject a little by saying. "Well we will certainly consider it Evelyn. Ashley is a sweet young lady. But first, I have some questions I just can't seem to figure out the answer to." Evelyn looked at Tom very seriously and said. "I'm not trying to replace your daughter Tom Carpenter. Please remember that. Now, what questions do you have for me?

Tom asked. "How is all this possible? I didn't know you before. And now we continue like old friends. I only knew you when I was in the coma; not here in real life." Evelyn replied. "Real life huh... It doesn't matter how or where we met Tom Carpenter. What matters is that we did. What matters is you and Kristi are back together again."

Tom continued as Kristi just sat still and listened. "It just doesn't seem real. It's like it was all a dream, but I remember every piece of it." Evelyn replied. "Sometimes a dream becomes a memory when it changes who you are Tom Carpenter. Did you know that?" Tom replied. "I never in my life heard such a thing." Evelyn smiled and said. "Just cause you haven't heard it doesn't mean it isn't true." Tom just shook his head a little and asked. "How did the wooden nickels come back with me? Kristi found them in my hand while I was in the coma. How is that possible?"

Evelyn looked at Kristi and saw that she wanted to know as well. Evelyn said to them. "Those nickels are very powerful. They are the memory that changed you. They are the bridge from this world to the next. You're daughter had to give them to you. She had to if so she could find her way back to you." Kristi said to Evelyn. "I can't explain how they got in Tom's hand, but I don't like what you're saying." Kristi started to tear up as she said. "Our daughter is dead. She's not coming back."

Evelyn saw the pain Kristi was feeling and Tom didn't say anything. He just looked at Kristi and patiently waited for an answer from Evelyn who said to them. "Her body died, yes it did. But I can tell you both, she's closer to you now than she has been in a long time." There was a pause between them all for a moment until Kristi asked Evelyn. "Tom says you know a way we can see her. I don't know you like Tom does... But if you do know a way." Kristi's stopped speaking as tears began to run down her cheeks and Tom eyes began to swell too. Kristi continued, saying as she put her hands against her face. "I want to see my daughter again."

Evelyn sighed heavily, looked at Kristi and Tom and said. "That's why I'm here today." Tom looked at Evelyn with a confused look and asked. "I thought you were here to talk to us about Ashley?" Evelyn held her coffee cup up to her lips concealing her grin as she said to Tom with a low voice. "You just don't listen Tom Carpenter." Evelyn took a sip of her coffee while Tom and Kristi looked at each shaking their heads as if they were suggesting the old woman was talking nonsense.

Before they continued with their conversation, something in the living area caught Kristi's eye since she was facing that direction. Ashley had came out of Amy's room and was standing in the living area with her arms wrapped around the skinny teddy bear. Tom and Evelyn were facing Kristi and saw that she was looking at something. Evelyn just smiled real big. Even with her back turned, she knew what Kristi was looking at.

Tom turned and when he saw Ashley holding the bear it hurt him a little; but he done well not to let it be heard in his voice when he said to Ashley. "You like that teddy bear?" Ashley looked at Tom and Kristi who both had the look of heartbreak on their faces and she responded, saying. "Skinny was my favorite."

CHAPTER 14

Upon hearing Ashley's words, Kristi let out a slight yelp as she gasped and covered her mouth with her hands. She knew there was no way Ashley could know the teddy bear's name. And Ashley referring to it as her favorite had Kristi's mind wondering. She looked at Tom hoping he would fill her in. Tom looked at Kristi for just a moment, but turned his attention to Evelyn who was just sitting there with a smile. Eventually she said to Tom with a low voice. "I already told you."

Tom's thoughts went back to when Evelyn said to him. "You have to trick them, because they feel they belong there." Tom remembered the vision he had of Evelyn and Amy standing by Ashley's bed in the hospital. Then Evelyn's most recent words about not trying to replace his daughter rang loud in his head. Tom looked very seriously but also questioningly at Evelyn. The old woman who was still smiling could see Tom was figuring it out. She didn't say anything, but rather she slowly gave Tom a wink.

Tom looked back to Ashley who was standing in the living area and looking at him. He slowly reached into his pocket and clinched his hand tight around the wooden nickels as he said. "Ashley... I'm glad you like that teddy bear." Tom looked at Kristi whose eyes were widened all the way as she waited to see what was going to happen.

Tom turned back to face Ashley and saw that she was getting teary eyed and still holding the bear. Tom asked her with a very calm voice. "Can I have another hug sweetie?" Ashley's breathing got faster and faster and the tears in her eyes started to streak down her cheeks. Ashley said to him with her little broken up voice. "I only take wooden nickels." Tom's hand trembled as he held it out and opened it revealing the two wooden nickels. Tom said to her over the lump in his throat and lightly gritted teeth. "I have two, Amy."

Ashley unwrapped her arms from the teddy bear and was holding by one leg down at her side. She said to Tom just one word he wanted to hear as she began to cry at the same time. "Daddy." The girl went to Tom and threw her arms around his neck with no concern for the wooden nickels he held.

Kristi jumped up from her chair when Ashley said the word daddy, and met her at Tom's side. When Ashley wrapped her arms around Tom; Kristi fell to her knees beside Tom's chair and leaned in to hug both of them. Ashley reached her right arm out and wrapped it around her mother for the first time in a very long time.

Kristi was quick to say to the little girl. "Oh God Amy... I love you so much baby girl." Even though Amy was in the body of Ashley; Tom and Kristi no longer saw her as Ashley. They could only see Amy even though she was in the form of Ashley. Amy said to her mom. "I love you too mommy. I've missed you and dad so much." Tom had his chin resting on Amy's shoulder as he just indulged in the moment and smiled at Evelyn. No one was happier than Tom to have his family back together.

It was a happy sad moment with a lot of emotion attached to it. Even old Evelyn Murray had to wipe her eyes but never quit smiling as she said. "Welcome home Carpenter family. Welcome home."

Evelyn broke the moment when she reached into her bag and pulled out the item wrapped with brown paper. The other three looked to see what she was doing. Tom and Kristi never took at least one hand off of their daughter who was in the form of Ashley. Evelyn never said anything but unwrapped her gift. It was the circular wooden portrait of Tom and Kristi with Ashley. The same one that caused a lot of problems in the family before.

Kristi saw it and said. "She knew the whole time." Evelyn got up out of her chair and took the portrait with her as she stood by the two foot blank wall at one side of the opening between the kitchen and living area. There was a nail sticking out of that wall where an old painting used to hang.

Evelyn hung the portrait up and said in response to Kristi's statement. "Yes. She knew." Tom said out loud but not directed at anyone. "I need to apologize to her." Ashley quickly turned to face Evelyn with a very unique and secretive smile on her face. Evelyn winked at the girl and said to Tom. "After all we've done together Tom Carpenter; you would think an old woman could get a hug. Unless you think I have the leprosy or something."

Tom laughed a little and let go of Kristi and Ashley. Kristi didn't let go of Ashley at all. Instead she now had both her arms around the girl as she watched Tom. Once Tom got stood up, Evelyn continued by saying. "I'm even willing to pay for it Tommy." Tom stopped dead in his tracks and watched as Evelyn held out a single wooden nickel. Tom looked at it and said. "The third sliver."

Evelyn grew slightly emotional and said. "Yes, I made a third. And I hoped that come the day I gave it to you; you would understand. I was always there for you, even if you couldn't see it."

Tom and Kristi were both extremely surprised at the old woman's words. Tom wasn't sure what was going on, but he took the wooden nickel in his hand and gave the old woman a hug before he asked. "This isn't across the plane. You can't be who you're suggesting to be."

Evelyn replied. "I don't expect you to understand it all right now, but understand that I never quit being your mother." She turned to Kristi and said. "You told Tom you never met Evelyn Murray and that was true." Tom asked. "So when you said if my wife was going to bother you then you were going to bother me..." The old woman smiled and said. "It wasn't a bother to me to help you two. But no, it wasn't Evelyn either."

Tom was still very questioning until Ashley broke Kristi's grasp, walked over and hugged the old woman and said. "Thank you grandma, for everything." The old woman replied to the girl. "You're welcome sweetie. I told you they wouldn't believe it." Ashley looked at Tom and said. "Things and people are not always what they seem across the plane dad."

Tom asked the old woman. "Was it you the whole time?" The old woman replied. "Evelyn did help Tom. She helped a lot but she couldn't be there much because she was with her granddaughter." Tom shook his head a little and asked. "Why did you take this appearance? Why are you still like this? How are you still like this?" The old woman replied. "Would you have let me help in the beginning if I had come to you as your mother?"

Tom nodded his head and said. "I see your point, but how? How is it possible here?" The old woman grinned a little and said. "Evelyn is busy right now across the plane, she didn't want to leave herself so empty and vulnerable, so I entered her to come here. I had to Tommy. I had to so you would listen and trust me enough to see your daughter."

Tom said to her as he shook his head. "Well, however it is, thank you. I wish I only knew earlier. For what it's worth mom, I'm sorry for all the things I've done to hurt you." The old woman replied. "It's okay son. It all worked out here in the end." Kristi was still in disbelief and said. "If that really is you in there, then thank you Katie."

The old woman looked at both Tom and Kristi and said. "The offer still stands you know. It stands with permission from Evelyn. She is old. Too old to raise another child." Tom quickly wrapped his left arm around Ashley and said. "She is home."

Tom reached his right arm out to hug the old woman one more time, and he whispered to her. "I knew it was you... Only my mother calls me Tommy." Tom's words brought tears to the old woman's eyes and she said to him "Yet you trusted me?" Tom replied with a slight grin. "I've been mad at you, but mad doesn't mean I couldn't trust you." Tom's mother who was in Evelyn Murray's body said to him. "I love you son."

After their moment, the old woman said to all the others. "I hate to leave, but I'm afraid I must. There is somewhere I need to be twenty minutes ago." Kristi quickly said to correct the old woman. "You mean in twenty minutes." The old woman said to her with a serious look on her face. "No. I said it right. I have to be somewhere twenty minutes ago."

Kristi and Tom just looked at each other with a confused look and Tom said to the old woman. "Come back anytime. Though in your regular appearance next time. And tell Evelyn we all said thank you." Kristi walked over and gave the old woman a long hug and said to her. "Thank you for helping us, all of us." The old woman said to them. "You all enjoy your time together. Cherish every moment... Now I really have to get going."

Tom stepped out of the way and walked the old woman to the door. After he opened the door and the old woman stepped out, Tom said to her. "Love you mom, and I'm sorry for everything." The old woman took a deep breath turned and said. "Don't be sorry son. You rest now, Tom Carpenter." Tom smiled from ear to ear as he heard her say his full name as Evelyn

Murray had always done. Just as he was about to shut the door, something caught his attention. Tom took a step closer to the opening and held his face to the sky and closed his eyes one more time. As he stood there, he began to smile and then laugh. His mother said to him. "Smell the rain son. She is home."

Tom took a final deep breath and said his final goodbye to his mother before he shut the door to be with his girls Kristi and Amy.

Twenty minutes earlier in the brick church at the end of town, the whole town seemed to be gathered inside. Down the long red carpeted aisle between the pews resting before the pulpit; were two identical brown colored with forest designed sided caskets. At the pulpit the town preacher Paul Thorton who was an elderly man was finishing his sermon by saying. "Tom Carpenter and Kristi Carpenter dying only minutes apart is testament of God's mercy; and further proof of his mysterious works. But let us rejoice in the remembrance that these two people who loved each other will not suffer anymore. They can rest now with their daughter they lost all those years ago, and finally be at peace."

The preacher held a short prayer before he started the viewing by saying. "We will start the viewing with Tom's mother Katie Carpenter and then work down the aisles from there." Katie Carpenter stood up. She was a square shouldered woman who stood nearly six feet tall and built strong like a female fighter even though she was in her sixties. She was wearing a full length long sleeved black dress which didn't do much to hide her strong body she acquired from all the woodworking. Her facial features slightly resembled Tom's in that she had deep set eyes and had a look that demanded respect.

Katie walked up to the casket that held her son as she carried something clenched in her hand. She leaned over, kissed Tom Carpenter on the head and whispered to his body. "One can't live if the other doesn't survive. You rest now with your family my son, Tom Carpenter." Katie leaned up a little and put the third wooden nickel under Tom's hands that were folded on his chest. Then she said with a whisper. "Give it back when I join you Tommy."

Katie walked over to Kristi's casket, leaned in and whispered to Kristi's body.

"Welcome home Kristi Carpenter. Take care of my son and granddaughter for me." Then Katie laid her hands on Kristi's for just a moment before she turned to leave.

Katie walked out of the church like the strong willed independent woman she was. She had her head held high and shoulders up square. Once she was outside, she got in her pickup truck and left. It wasn't her style to stick around and let everyone pat her on the back and cry on her shoulder. Her demeanor was what made half the towns' people think she was crazy, and the other half show complete respect when talking to her.

The other people in the church were making their rounds around the caskets and meeting outside to talk about how strange it was that both Tom and Kristi's hearts gave out at the same time. They didn't understand that Tom and Kristi were soul mates and couldn't live without each other. Even across the plane, both would have died if the other didn't survive. For Tom, Kristi and Amy, the power and memories tied to the two wooden nickels was enough to join all three of them in their home somewhere across the plane.

Later that year, just as the leaves were starting to change. Evelyn Murray was walking through the town cemetery. She looked just as she always did except she was wearing a solid black dress under her old grey poncho. Her long dark grey and streaky black hair was the same as well as it hung down on the sides of her face.

Around a hundred feet away from her, three young boys were standing on the road that ran through the cemetery making fun of Evelyn. They were leaning over and walking slow to mimic how she walked. And they were making jokes about her going to wake the dead and all sorts of things boys do. Evelyn wasn't paying any attention to them. She had something else on her mind she felt she needed to do. That was to say a final goodbye to the man she had come to know.

Soon she came to a grave that had fresh young grass growing on it, but was noticeably a newer grave. Evelyn stood before a long headstone that had three cement vases on top of it. On the front were the names and dates. Tom Carpenter June 5, 1956- beside his was Kristi Carpenter November 21, 1958- and Amy Carpenter April 12, 1976-. None of them had an end date. At the bottom of the headstone were the words. "Love has no ending."

Evelyn kneeled down and rested her right hand on top of the headstone as it helped balance her. She kept the staff in her left hand for extra support. She said while kneeling there. "Just thought I would stop by while I was out today." Evelyn looked around for a minute and looked to the three boys who were poking fun at her and she said. "Those ornery shits; if it wasn't for them I would be mighty bored now days." Evelyn patted the top of the headstone and said with a smile. "You rest now with your family my good friend, Tom Carpenter. I have to go scare some children. It's how I get my exercise."

Evelyn stood up slow using the staff and headstone to help her. Once she got on her feet she started walking in the direction of the three boys who were still talking about her casting spells, and stirring a large cauldron. When Evelyn got half way to the boys she saw they were getting ready to run. So she pointed her staff at them and yelled. "I'll turn you three into frogs and fry your little legs!"

The three boys took off running and yelling at the same time. Old Evelyn stood her staff back upright so she could lean on it as she turned to face the Carpenter's headstone. Evelyn smiled that familiar old ornery smile and gave Tom Carpenter a wink one last time.

THE END

ACROSS THE PLANE

(Evelyn Murray)

Coming soon!

Made in the USA
Columbia, SC
04 June 2019